When You've Been Blessed

(Feels Like Heaven)

I0552708

Adrienne Thompson

Pink Cashmere Publishing

USA

Edited by: Alyndria Mooney

Cover Design by: Adrienne Thompson

First Printing 2012

Copyright © 2012 Adrienne Thompson

ISBN: 0983756945

ISBN-13: 978-0-9837569-4-1

Also by Adrienne Thompson

BluesDay

Been So Long

Coming in 2012

Lovely Blues (BluesDay Book Two)

See Me

Praise for *BluesDay*:

"...the kind of book you can read through in one relaxing evening and enjoy every moment thereof..."
Books4Tommorow – 5 stars

"...If you're looking for a good read--this is it..."
Author Nakia Laushaul – 4 stars

Praise for *Been So Long*:

"...a good story, with good characters, and after finishing the story I wanted more..."
Anonymous Barnes and Noble reviewer – 5 stars

"...I was very impressed by the creative original story line, the diversity and colorful characters..."
pinkchameleonrn (Barnes and Noble reviewer) – 5 stars

"...When I started reading, I didn't want to put it down..."
M. Nesby (Amazon reviewer) – 5 stars

To my Father in Heaven, You never cease to amaze me. Thank You for Your faithful and unconditional love, Your daily mercies, and Your true awesomeness.

To my earthly father, Dr. Joe Hargrove, thanks for being my daddy. I love you.

To my beautiful grandson, Christopher Ethan Mooney. Gigi loves you!

If you've ever been hurt by someone you loved, this one's for you. May you find healing and restoration, and may your latter be greater than your former.

Love never fails…

1 Corinthians 13:8

Soundtrack

"Hallelujah Praise" by Cece Winans
"You Don't Know" by Kierra "Kiki" Sheard
"I Need You Now" by Smokie Norful
"Heaven Knows" by Deitrick Haddon
"Heard A Word" by Michelle Williams
"Let Go" by Dewayne Woods
"I'll Make It" by Hezekiah Walker
"Up Above My Head" by God's Property (Kirk Franklin's Nu Nation)
"Shackles" by Mary Mary
"No, Never" by Kierra "Kiki" Sheard
"Go Through" by Evelyn Turrentine-Agee
"Bread of Heaven" by Fred Hammond
"Moving Forward" by Israel Houghton
"Trading My Sorrows" by Darrell Evans
"Made Me Glad" by Hillsong
"It Ain't Over" by Maurette Brown Clark
"Glorious" by Martha Munizzi
"Grateful" by Hezekiah Walker
"Celebrate" by Smokie Norful
"Livin'" by The Clark Sisters
"I'll Take You There" by Bebe and Cece Winans
"Look At Me" by John Tillery
"Desperate" by Fireflight
"Just Wanna Say" by Israel Houghton
"Love" by God's Property (Kirk Franklin's Nu Nation)
"Imagine Me" by Kirk Franklin
"That's What I Believe" by Donnie McClurkin
"Faith" by God's Property (Kirk Franklin's Nu Nation)
"Healed" by Donald Lawrence
"Complete" by LaShun Pace

1

"Hallelujah Praise"

"BROTHERS AND SISTERS, THIS IS WHAT YOU'VE BEEN waiting for! Our special guest for tonight's program, the Anointed Woman of God, the lovely Ms. Tonya Langford-Hill!"

I squeezed my eyes shut and prayed for a fresh anointing just as I did before every performance. I stood to the side of the platform in that huge church and listened as the musicians began to play, "Truly Blessed". It was one of The Langford Sisters' biggest hits. Although the group had disbanded almost twenty years earlier, it was still a crowd favorite and I always included it in my performances. After a little over a minute of instrumental music, I stepped onto the platform and took my place in the center.

The church was full of worshippers. I smiled at the people as they stood from their seats, swayed to the up-beat tempo, and raised their hands. I clapped my hands before removing the microphone from its stand and singing the opening lines of the song…

"Amen, hallelujah!
I know I'm free.
King Jesus, the Messiah
Has liberated me!
No longer bound in chains
Free to be forever changed

Let me tell you, it feels good to be
Truly, Truly Blessed!"

I put my hand on my hip, belted out the lyrics, and smiled as the sound of the congregation singing along filled my ears. For the next two hours I sang praises to God.

This was the last performance of a three-week tour, and although I loved singing for the Lord, I was more than eager to get back home to my family. My husband, Reverend Apollo Hill, was the senior pastor of the Christ Fellowship Church, one of the largest non-denominational churches in Little Rock. With several active ministries, Apollo was unable to travel with me as he had earlier in our marriage. He'd been the love of my life for many years, and we were absolutely perfect for each other. I missed him so much and I couldn't wait to be back in my own church, cheering him on from the front pew.

I ended the performance with an altar call—personally praying with several people. I was so pleased and excited to have been able to lead two or three non-believers to Christ. I talked with a few people and even had a couple of impromptu counseling sessions. It always amazes me the pain and sorrow that so many people experienced. Bad decisions had ruined so many lives; it was mind-blowing. One lady in particular shared with me that she was struggling in her marriage. She told me about her husband's numerous infidelities and how she felt that her desperate prayers weren't being heard. I assured her that they were and that God does things in His own timing. As I held her hand and tried to offer her some comfort and reassurance, I thanked God that I'd never been in her shoes.

I hugged well wishers and spoke with the church's pastor before leaving with my small entourage (a personal assistant, make-up artist, and hair-dresser) for the hotel. My flight home from St. Louis was scheduled to leave at eight in the morning, and I would need to pack and be in bed early in order to make it to the airport on time.

I climbed into the limo, settled into the seat, closed my eyes, and breathed a sigh of relief. I loved singing, but I was glad the tour was over. Pasting on a permanent smile and trying to appear energetic at all times was exhausting. I poured myself a glass of champagne and sipped all the way to the hotel. I treasured my quiet time after a performance.

Back at the hotel, I made my usual nightly phone calls—my mother, my daughter, and my husband. My mom answered the phone and gave me a quick report on my ailing father. I was worried about him, but Mama said he was holding up pretty well. Mom and I prayed over the phone together and after our call ended, I dialed my daughter's cell phone number. Rebekah was attending college in Tennessee, and she was always happy to talk to me. We had a special bond, and I adored her.

I dialed her number and listened as it went straight to voicemail. *That's odd,* I thought, *maybe she forgot to charge it.* I shrugged and then hung up and dialed my home number.

"Hello," Apollo's familiar voice said. I smiled.

"Hello, my king. This is your wife," I said.

"Mmm, a melody to my ears. How are you, darling?"

"Tired, but blessed."

"I know that's right. Blessed you definitely are. Me and AJ been missing you. You're home tomorrow, right?"

I smiled at hearing my son's name. AJ was my youngest child and he was definitely a mama's boy. "Yes, sir, and I can't wait. I've missed y'all, too, and I've missed sleeping in my own bed."

"Well, it's been a lonely bed without you, my dear. *Very lonely.*"

I opened my mouth to reply, but then I heard what sounded like a giggle in the background. "Uh, is that the TV? What are you watching? I thought I heard someone laughing," I said.

"Huh…what, baby? Hold on a minute, you're breaking up."

I held the phone, but it was more than a minute before Apollo returned. "Sorry about that, baby. Now, what were you saying?"

I frowned. *What is going on?* "Um, I thought I heard someone laughing. Was it the TV?"

"Oh, yeah. I just turned it off." He yawned loudly into the phone.

Something felt off. If I didn't know any better, I might've thought he was lying. *Come on, Tonya. Get a grip. This is your husband you're talking about here.* "You must've been busy today. You sound tired," I said.

"Mm, yes, I have. Been working with the youth department at the church. You know how tiring those kids can be."

"I hear you. I'm pretty tired myself."

"You should be! Out there working hard for the Lord. Get some rest; you'll need it because we've got to make up for lost time. I'll see you in the morning."

I smiled again. "Okay, I love you."

"Love you, too."

Still smiling, I hung up the phone and began to pack my bag. Afterwards I showered and prepared for bed. As I laid my head on the pillow, I closed my eyes and said a prayer of thanksgiving before settling into a peaceful sleep. It was foolish of me to doubt Apollo. He was a good man and a great husband. God is good, and so was my life. I didn't think it could get any better.

2

"You Don't Know"

I BREATHED A SIGH OF RELIEF AS I DE-BOARDED THE PLANE
at the airport in Little Rock. I loved singing for God more than
anything in the world, but I also loved my family, and I was more
than ready for some quality time with my hubby. As I made my way
to the luggage claim area, Apollo stood waiting for me as usual. He
greeted me with a hug and a kiss on the cheek before retrieving my
bags for me and leading me out to his glossy, black Chrysler 300.

Dressed in light brown slacks and a navy blue dress shirt, my
husband was visual perfection. From the moment I met him, I was
captivated by his looks. He stood head and shoulders above most
men, and to say that he was handsome would be an understatement.
His athletic build always caught the eye of every woman in the
room. Add all of that to his natural charisma, commanding presence,
and vast knowledge of the Word of God, and you have one of the
most beloved pastors in Central Arkansas.

I adored him. Nothing made me more proud than being Mrs. Apollo Hill. I delighted in being his first lady, both at church and at home. After all, my sisters and I had been groomed to be pastor's wives almost since birth. I was the only one of us who'd won the prize, though.

I smiled as I settled into the passenger's seat of the car and fastened my seatbelt.

"Where's AJ?" I asked.

Apollo started the car and said, "Not sure. I think he had plans with Denesha."

I nodded. "Oh, okay. I guess they're really getting serious, huh?"

Apollo laughed. "Tonya, he's *eighteen*. I doubt if he's anywhere close to getting serious about anyone. Eighteen is too young to be settling down. He needs to live life."

I raised my eyebrows. "Oh really? I was only eighteen and you were only twenty when we got married, remember?"

He glanced at me and smiled. "But you were the beautiful Tonya Langford, the angel with the golden voice. How was I supposed to let you slip away?"

I reached over and rubbed his cheek with my finger. "You're pretty special yourself, Rev. Hill. I would've been a fool to let you pass me by."

His smile widened. "Aw girl, I'm just a little old country preacher. Born and raised right here in Arkansas."

"That's just the kind of man for me. You know what? I'm gonna fix you a big dinner tonight."

He raised his eyebrows. "Really? Aren't you tired from your trip?"

"Yeah, I am but I missed my husband. I wanna do something nice for him."

"You already did something nice for me. You made it home safely."

I leaned over the console and kissed my husband's cheek. "I love you, Rev. Hill."

"I love you, too."

♪♪♪

I peered into the oven and checked on the stuffed bell peppers I'd prepared. I planned to complete Apollo's favorite meal by adding loaded mashed potatoes and fresh green beans to the menu. I smiled as I inhaled the heavenly scent flowing from the oven, then walked over to the island situated in the middle of the spacious kitchen and continued to dice the potatoes. As I worked, I cheerfully hummed along with a tune on the radio. I was having an absolutely wonderful day.

In the midst of my bliss, I heard my cell phone vibrate against the kitchen table. I took a seat at the table and picked up my phone. The screen read: *unavailable.*

"Hello?" I answered.

Click.

I frowned as I held the phone in my hand and was startled when it began to vibrate again. This time the screen indicated that it was my daughter.

"Hello?"

"Hey, Ma. Sorry I missed your call last night."

"Mmhmm," I replied absently. My mind was still on the hang-up call.

"Ma, you ok? You sound a little preoccupied."

"Hmm? Oh, yes, I'm fine. But I was a little worried when I couldn't reach you. Everything alright?"

"Um, yes ma'am. I was in a friend's room, studying. You're back home now?"

"Yeah. I'm cooking dinner. How's school?"

"Okay. Got an A on my English paper."

I smiled. "Good! You always make me and your father so proud."

"Well, I try, but I'm not perfect, Ma."

"Oh, you're as perfect as they come. Always being so responsible and doing what's right." The doorbell rang. "Hey Beka, let me call you back. Someone's at the door."

"Oh, okay."

She sounded like something was on her mind; but then again, Rebekah would worry about the smallest of things. One time she called me in tears because she got a "B" on a test. I shook my head as I hung up the phone and headed through the huge house to the front door.

"Who is it?" I called through the door, my hand on the dead bolt lock.

"Um, Lisa—from church."

Lisa...Lisa... I thought. *I don't remember a Lisa.*

I peeked through the peep hole but couldn't see anyone. "Who'd you say?"

"Lisa, Mrs. Hill. Gwen Donley's daughter."

I nodded. Gwen was the church secretary. "Oh, ok." I unlocked the door and greeted the young lady with my "First Lady" smile. I had to be in character at all times, whether I wanted to or not. It just comes with the territory. "Well, come on in."

The young lady, who was short and thin, nodded and slowly entered the house. She eyed the foyer from top to bottom taking in everything from the spotless marble floors to the mahogany molding.

Lisa said, "Your house is beautiful."

"Well, thank you. Come on in and have a seat."

I led the young lady to the formal living room and offered her a seat on the plush white sofa. After taking a seat beside her, I said, "How can I help you?"

She was hesitant as she said, "Well, I was actually hoping to talk with Rev. Hill. Is he here?"

I shook my head. "No, he's not. Is it something I can help you with?"

Lisa dropped her eyes and shook her head. "I don't see how you can help me. I'm in trouble, and only Rev. Hill can fix it."

I frowned. I knew that the members loved Apollo, but this girl was acting like he was God. How could only Apollo fix her trouble? "Lisa, why don't you tell me what's wrong and then I can discuss it with my husband if need be. Let me help you."

She peered up at me. "Well, I've been seeing this guy, and things have been getting kinda serious."

I nodded. "Okay, and…"

Lisa began to tear up. "And, well, I just found out today that I'm pregnant. I'm so scared. I haven't even told my mama yet."

These young girls are always getting themselves in trouble. I'm so glad that my daughter has a good head on her shoulders. I reached over and grasped Lisa's hand. "Honey, how old are you?"

Tears streamed down Lisa's face as she said, "Eighteen."

Lord, have mercy. "And the father? Does he go to school with you?"

Lisa shook her head. "Oh no, ma'am. He's older, much older. And he's married."

Oh, Lord. What kind of man would take advantage of a young girl like this, I wondered. *She's as green as grass.*

"Sweetie, I understand what you're going through." That was a lie, but it was my standard counseling spiel. I continued with, "This is definitely a difficult situation for you, but remember, nothing is too difficult for God. You need to tell the father. But you also need to tell your mother. She can be a great support to you. Most of all, Lisa, you need to pray. Would you like for me to pray with you now?"

Lisa nodded. "Would you do that?"

I smiled. "Of course. Bow your head." I closed my eyes and began to pray for Lisa, her mother, and her unborn child. When I was finished, I hugged Lisa and after exchanging phone numbers with her, walked her to the front door. Lisa thanked me and left. I finished preparing dinner and a little over an hour later, was joined by Apollo at the dining room table.

"This is delicious, baby. I feel privileged that the world-famous Tonya Langford-Hill has prepared dinner for me. Now, what did I do to deserve this?" Apollo said with a wide toothy grin on his face. Deep dimples accented his cheeks.

I returned his smile. "Aw now, around here I'm just Mrs. Apollo Hill, the pastor's wife. And you are the best husband a woman could ask for. *That's* why you deserve this. I wish I could spoil you more often."

"Oh, but you must travel the world with your ministry. That's what God's called you to do. I miss you when you're gone, but I know it's to further the kingdom."

"You see? That's what I'm talking about. You understand me, and you accept the work I've been called to do. How did I get so lucky when so many others get stuck dealing with these horrible men?"

Apollo frowned. "Whoa, where'd that come from? Kind of heavy for dinner conversation, isn't it?"

I sighed. "I'm sorry. It's just that one of the members came by and talked to me earlier today. She was a young girl, really sweet.

Naïve, but sweet. Some dirty old married man's gotten her in trouble. It just breaks my heart. Someone needs to talk to these girls."

Apollo scooped up a healthy portion of mashed potatoes. "Really? Who was she?"

"Um, her name was Lisa. She's the secretary's daughter."

Apollo began to cough as if he'd choked on his food. I reached across the table and handed him his glass of water.

"You okay, baby? Too much pepper in the potatoes?" I asked.

Apollo caught his breath and said, "I think something went down the wrong way." He cleared his throat. "Um, what did she say, you know, about this guy?"

"Nothing other than he's married, and now she's pregnant by him. Apollo, she's just eighteen. *A baby*. What kind of dirty old man would do that? He must be a pedophile."

Apollo frowned. "I wouldn't go so far as to say a pedophile, honey. Eighteen is the age of adulthood. That would be like calling me a pedophile since you were eighteen when we married."

I shook my head. "Sweetie, this is hardly the same thing. You weren't some adulterous married man taking advantage of a young innocent girl."

Apollo shrugged. "Well, baby, you don't know the whole story. Maybe she seduced him or something."

"Seduced him? Are you saying that a grown man with a wife can't control himself any better than that? Come on now, Rev. Hill.

You can't be serious. Besides, that little girl didn't have a sexy bone in her frail little body. And she was so timid."

He cleared his throat again. "I just mean that no one person is totally to blame. At eighteen a person knows right from wrong."

"Well, you're right, but I just still feel so sorry for her. She seemed so alone and so scared."

He shook his head. "That's my baby. Always taking everyone at face value. You never know the truth until you know the whole story, Tonya. That girl might have been playing you for sympathy."

I shrugged. "Well, that's true. Anyway, let's just enjoy our dinner, and then we can have dessert."

Apollo smiled. "And what's for dessert?"

"What do you think?"

3

"I Need You Now"

I LAY ASLEEP, SECURE IN MY HUSBAND'S ARMS, WHEN HIS cell phone rang. By then, I was used to late night calls from church members reporting that a loved one was sick or had entered the hospital or had passed away. I even kept an outfit hanging in the closet in case Apollo and I had to make an unexpected trip in the middle of the night. But the calls usually came to the house phone. Only church officials or family members had his cell number. I lifted my head up from his chest and shook his shoulder.

"Apollo, your phone's ringing," I said.

"Hmm?" he responded groggily.

"Honey, your phone's ringing. You want me to get it?"

He shook his head and rubbed his eyes. "No, I'll get it. No sense in both of us having to break our rest."*My rest is already broken*, I thought.

Apollo kissed my forehead then sat up on the side of the bed to pull on his boxers and a t-shirt as he answered the phone.

"Hello?" he said. He listened to the caller for a moment and then said, "Alright, hold on a minute."

He stood and left the room. I lay back down and closed my eyes but found it impossible to fall back to sleep. My mind was reeling, wondering who was on the phone and what had happened. Finally, I sat up on the side of the bed and wrapped my robe around the fleshy curves of my body. I ran my hand through the soft twists on my head and slid my feet into my slippers.

I headed out of the room, having decided to get a glass of water from the kitchen. I walked down the hall towards the winding staircase and as I passed our son AJ's room, noticed that his light was on. *I guess he finally made it home,* I thought as I peeped through the slightly open door. It was Apollo, not AJ, who was in the room. Apollo was sitting on the side of AJ's bed with his back to the door having a rather hushed conversation on the phone. I stood there for a moment and then told myself not to eavesdrop. *He'll tell me about it when he hangs up. He always does.*

I continued to the kitchen, fixed a glass of water, and headed back up the stairs. This time when I passed by AJ's room, I could hear Apollo raising his voice. I stopped by the door and listened.

"Don't you ever call me at this time of night again, you understand? And you sure as hell better not come to my house. We'll deal with this later," he said in a harsh whisper.

I raised my eyebrows and wondered who he was talking to and

what he was talking about. I stood there for a few more seconds, but he lowered his voice and I couldn't make out what he was saying. Not wanting to get caught eavesdropping, I headed to the bedroom and settled back into the bed. A few minutes later, Apollo returned to our bedroom, climbed into the bed, and spooned himself behind me.

"Who was that?" I asked.

"Nobody, one of the deacons about some program. Go back to sleep, baby."

I frowned. "A deacon at this time of night? Which deacon?"

"Yeah, I'm gonna have a talk with him in the morning." He only half answered my question.

He snuggled closer to me and kissed my shoulder. I opened my mouth to reply but then decided against it. I was pretty positive that Apollo was lying, but I didn't want to argue. We never argued, and I liked it that way. I closed my eyes and tried to sleep, but couldn't. That phone call and what I'd heard Apollo saying to the caller was all I could think of. I lay there wide awake for what felt like hours listening to Apollo's breathing and finally, having waited as long as I could, slipped out of the bed and quietly walked around to pick Apollo's phone up from the night table.

I tipped out into the hallway. I shook my head and thought, *Lord, I can't believe I'm checking his phone. We've been married for twenty years, and I'm checking his phone like some kind of jealous crazy person.*

"I'm not doing this," I whispered to myself.

I turned back towards our bedroom door but couldn't make myself move. *Okay, I'll just check it and see that it was one of the deacons like he said, and then I can get some sleep.* I took a deep breath and then clicked the button on Apollo's phone until his call log popped up. The last call received did not have a name programmed with it, but for some reason, it looked familiar to me. I stood there for a moment—then it dawned on me where I'd seen the number. I quickly walked down the stairs and into the living room. I picked up a piece of paper from the coffee table. On it was Lisa Donley's number from our counseling session earlier. I closed my eyes and then held the paper up next to the phone. Just as I'd suspected, the numbers were the same.

Why was Lisa calling him in the middle of the night? Better yet, what was she doing with his personal cell number? And why had Apollo lied about who was on the phone? I stood there for a minute or so and tried to decide whether or not I should confront Apollo about the phone call. As it turned out, I didn't have to. As I stood there contemplating my next move, Apollo's voice shocked me out of my thoughts.

"What are you doing down here? I missed you." He asked in his booming baritone voice.

I spun around, still holding his phone in my hand. I stood there and stared at him, but did not answer his question.

"And what are you doing with my phone?" he added with a frown.

"What were you doing on the phone with that girl?" I countered.

"What? Who? You been checking my phone, Tonya?" Apollo said, raising his voice a little.

"Answer the question, Apollo. You know what girl I'm talking about. I know this is her number because she gave it to me when she was here."

He shook his head. "I can't believe that after twenty years of marriage, you are actually checking up on me. Come on, Tonya. This is ridiculous."

I shut my eyes tightly. "Well, you put me in this position. Why did you lie about who was on the phone? How did that girl get your number?"

"Tonya, is this for real? You think I got something going on with that girl? You know better than that. Come on and let's go back to bed." He reached for my arm and I snatched away from him.

"Apollo, you haven't answered one question. Why did you lie?!"

"Okay, okay. She got my number from her mother. She needed to talk about her trouble, so I talked to her. That's all."

"Then why did you tell her not to call you or come by here?"

"I never said any such thing."

He was lying. I couldn't believe that he was standing there looking me straight in the eye and lying! He'd never lied to me before, had he?

"Oh my G—you're lying! You said it. *I heard you*, Apollo."

"What?! Now you're eavesdropping on my conversations?

What's gotten into you?"

I folded my arms across my chest. "Maybe the better question is, 'Who've *you* gotten in to?' Are you her baby's father?"

He laughed. "What?! Are you serious? Didn't we just make love a few hours ago? Did that feel like I've been with someone else?"

I dropped my eyes. Apollo's lovemaking always made me feel like I was the only woman he wanted, like he'd bottled up all of his passion and only released it when I returned home. Even after twenty years, he couldn't seem to get enough of me.

"Did it?" he repeated.

I shifted my weight on my feet and then looked up at Apollo. "Well, no, but why lie? You've never lied to me before."

Apollo moved closer to me and placed his hands on my shoulders. "She asked me to keep it confidential. She told me who the father was, and I knew if I told you she'd talked to me, you'd want to know what we talked about. I was just trying to respect her privacy," he said softly.

I shook my head and sighed. "I'm sorry. I don't know what's going on with me. I guess I'm out on the road so much; I just worry about things between us sometimes."

He smiled down at me and then kissed me softly, sending a spark through me. It was amazing that he still had such an effect on me. "I love you, baby. There's no one else I want in this world. Now come on back to bed. We got church in the morning."

I nodded. "Okay."

As we began to walk back to our bedroom, Apollo's phone rang again. I had forgotten that I was still holding it. I looked at it for a moment and then handed it to him. He looked at the screen and frowned.

"I don't know this number," he said. He pressed the button, accepted the call, and cautiously said, "Hello?"

I watched as he listened attentively to the voice on the other end. His eyes widened as he nodded and repeatedly said, "Okay." Finally, he hung up and then turned to me. "Well, it seems that our son is in jail."

I gasped. "WHAT?! What happened? Is he okay?"

"The officer said something about an assault and battery charge. I'll get dressed and go bail him out."

"O...okay. You want me to come?"

"No, stay here. I'll be back with him as soon as I can."

"Okay."

Ten minutes later, Apollo left for the police station and I sat in the living room with my Bible open. After reading a few scriptures, I knelt down in front of the sofa and began to pray for my family.

4

"Heaven Knows"

I SAT ON THE SOFA AND WAITED FOR APOLLO TO RETURN home with AJ. I'd prayed, cried, and paced the floor, filled with worry and concern for my only son. AJ had always been a pretty well-behaved child growing up. The trouble with him began at the beginning of the current school year—his senior year in high school. He turned eighteen over the summer and seemed to believe that he could do whatever he pleased. Late nights had become the norm for him, and I was almost sure he was drinking on a regular basis. Drugs weren't out of the question, either. I hadn't shared my concerns with Apollo. Sometimes I thought he could be a little too hard on AJ. While he doted on Rebekah, believing that she could do no wrong, he seemed to believe that AJ could do no right.

I heard a car door slam outside. I stood up from the sofa and walked toward the front door. The door opened and I watched as

Apollo shoved AJ into the house.

"What's going on? What happened?" I asked, looking from Apollo to AJ.

Apollo flung his keys on the table next to the front door and yelled, "This damn son of yours decided he'd get drunk and beat his girlfriend up. Had me down at that police station; it's embarrassing!"

I frowned. "Beat her up?" I turned to AJ. "Son, why would lay your hands on a woman? Haven't we taught you better than that? You've never seen your father lay a hand on me, *ever*."

AJ leaned against the wall and shook his head. "Yeah, Dad's a real stand-up guy, right? If you only knew the truth..." *He must be drunk.*

"What are you talking about, AJ?" I asked.

"You can't pay no attention to that boy. Can't you tell he's drunk?" Apollo said.

I turned to AJ and asked. "Have you been drinking?"

AJ nodded. "Well, yeah, I have, but that don't mean I don't know what I'm talking about. Your husband's a rotten dude and a fake-ass preacher."

Before I could respond, Apollo stepped closer to AJ and said, "Hey, you need to watch your mouth, boy. I don't care how old you are. I'm still your father and I will still whoop your tail!"

AJ waved his father away. "Whatever, man. You ain't father of the year, and you sho' ain't husband of the year. And you can try to whoop me, but I ain't gon' just stand here and take it."

Apollo lunged for AJ. I quickly stepped between them and placed my hand on AJ's chest.

"What's going on, AJ? What's gotten into to you? What are you talking about?" I said.

AJ looked as his father. "You gon' tell her or you want me to?" he asked.

I looked at Apollo. "What is he talking about?"

Silence.

"Someone tell me what's going on!" I shouted.

"Nothing, Tonya! THE BOY IS DRUNK! DAMN!" Apollo roared.

AJ backed away. "I might be drunk, but I know what you are, *Reverend Apollo Hill, Sr.* You're a liar and a cheater."

"You need to shut up, boy!" Apollo shouted as he lunged for AJ again.

AJ backed completely out of his reach. "Naw, this crap has gone on long enough!" AJ said. Then he turned towards me. "Mama, dude been cheating on you for years. I saw him one time when I was younger. You were gone on a tour, and he had some trick all up in y'all's room. He made me promise not to tell. But I'm grown now, and I'ma tell it all."

I turned and looked at Apollo. My head began to throb. "What's he talking about, Apollo?"

Apollo shook his head. "You gonna stand here and believe this drunk boy? You know he hates me. I'm sick of him. Rebekah's never disrespected me like this."

I took a deep breath and repeated myself as the throbbing in my head began to intensify. "Apollo, what is our son talking about? Did you have a woman in our house?"

"Ton—" Apollo began, but was interrupted by AJ.

"Oh, it was more than one. He does it all the time. Shoot, he a big-time church playa. Got a new flavor every month or so. He just had a girl my age up in here the other day. Hell, I was tryna holler at Lisa but Daddy Dearest beat me to it," AJ said.

I glared at Apollo. "Lisa?! So you *are* the baby's daddy?!"

AJ bucked his eyes. "Oh man, is ol' girl pregnant? Dang Pops, you ain't have enough sense to wrap it up? That's messed up."

Apollo pushed me out of his way, sending me to the floor, and pounced on AJ. I scrambled to my feet and grabbed Apollo from behind, finally pulling him off of our son. AJ stumbled to his feet, his nose bloodied by his father.

"*That's* where I got it from," he said pointing to his father.

I held onto Apollo as AJ walked past us.

"I'm outta here," AJ said and then walked out of the front door.

I watched him leave, then turned to Apollo and calmly said, "You need to leave."

He placed his hand on my arm, and I instantly snatched away from him. "Come on, baby. We need to talk about this," he said in a syrupy sweet voice.

"Talk about what? You fighting your own son like a mad man, or you cheating on me and knocking up a girl young enough to be your daughter? Because I just don't see how you can explain some mess like this."

"Look, the boy is drunk, baby. When he sobers up, you'll see he was lying."

I shook my head. "No, that boy is tormented. He's upset because he's had to keep this from me. He might be drunk, but drunk people are not known for lying, Apollo. If anything, the liquor gives them courage to tell the truth, and I believe him. Now, get out."

Apollo stood up straight and his expression changed. With a hard look on his face, he said, "No, I ain't going nowhere. This is my house, too."

"Fine, then I'll go."

Apollo smiled smugly. "Naw, you ain't going nowhere, and you know it."

"*Watch me.*" I grabbed my purse and stormed out of the house. I climbed into my silver BMW, laid my head against the steering wheel and cried, all the while wondering, *What just happened?*

♪♪♪

We slowly boarded the plane, and I sighed with relief when the pilot announced take-off. I rested the back of my head against the bucket seat. I glanced over at my son, who sat next to me. After leaving home, I'd found AJ at a friend's house and then booked a flight for both of us to Atlanta. It was spring break and I decided that we would spend some time at my mother's house. I hoped that the change of scenery would clear the cobwebs from my mind.

I closed my eyes and shook my head. I was still reeling from AJ's revelation. I'd often thought that maybe Apollo had been unfaithful to me, but with no evidence to support my hunch, I just pushed the notion to the back of my mind and ignored the red flags that were waving all over my house. After all, he was a preacher—a man of God. Surely he wouldn't do something like that. I'd seen him counsel couples and give them good, sound, Biblical advice that often saved their marriages. How could he possibly have done something that could destroy his *own* marriage?

I sighed and shifted in my seat. AJ looked over at me and grasped my hand.

"I'm sorry, Mama. If I hadn't been drinking, I probably wouldn't have told you that stuff. I know it hurt you," he said with concern in his eyes.

I shook my head. "No, I'm glad you told me. I needed to know. I just hate that you had to carry this around for so long. *I'm* sorry."

AJ frowned. "Naw, you ain't got nothing to be sorry for, Mama. Daddy is a messed up dude, up there preaching every Sunday and dogging you out time you walk out the door. I bet he up there preaching right now. Telling folks to live right and he living wrong. I hate him."

I looked AJ in the eye. "Don't feel that way. What your father did had nothing to do with you. Now, he shouldn't have made you keep his secret, but he's still your father, and for that alone he deserves your respect, you understand?"

AJ shrugged. "Yeah, I guess. But I ain't trying to see him no time soon."

"Okay, fair enough. I think we all need time to cool down. Tell me, did you really hit Denesha?"

AJ dropped his eyes and nodded. "Well, I kinda shoved her, really."

"Why?"

"We were arguing over some girl she thinks I'm messing around with. I was through talking, but she got in my face, pointing her finger and rolling her neck, and she got on my nerves, so I pushed her away. Then she swung at me. I didn't never really hit her, but I pushed her a couple of times and she fell. She got up all upset and started crying. I apologized but she wasn't tryna hear it. She called the cops, and well…you know the rest."

I shook my head. "Son, next time just walk away, okay? Nothing is worth you going to jail. Nothing and *no one*."

He nodded. "Yeah, well, ain't gon' be no next time. I'm done with that girl. She's crazy in the head, for real. Too jealous."

"Good. I love you, AJ. I just want the best for you."

"Love you, too, Mama."

After landing, we exited the airplane and headed through the terminal to rent a vehicle. Minutes later, we were weaving through the heavy Atlanta traffic, on our way to my parents' house in Buckhead.

5

"Heard a Word"

I PULLED THE RENTED SUV ONTO THE CIRCULAR DRIVEWAY in front of my parents' home. As I drew nearer, I began to feel a little better. I hadn't been home to visit in a year or so, and I really missed seeing my parents—especially my father. I was always his favorite daughter, although he'd never admitted it. I was sure that my sisters knew it, though.

Shortly after Apollo and I were married, he was named youth pastor at Christ Fellowship Church and had insisted that I leave The Langford Sisters, a musical group which consisted of me and my three sisters, Toi, Theresa, and Tennille. A few years later, Apollo became senior pastor at the church and I'd managed to carve out a very successful solo career. Between our busy careers and raising our two children, there hadn't been much time for family visits.

"I coulda drove," AJ said as I pulled the vehicle to a stop in front of the house. He was slumped in the passenger seat, peering out the side window.

I smiled over at him. "You don't know Atlanta, baby. I just didn't want you to have a wreck."

"Yeah, okay. But next time I wanna drive."

I nodded as we walked up to the front door. "We'll see."

I knocked and waited for someone to answer.

"Who is it?" a voice called through the door.

"Tonya," I said. I wasn't sure which of my sisters it was, but I knew it was one of them.

The door swung open to reveal my youngest sister, Tennille. Tennille was shorter and a little heavier than me, but we both possessed the same caramel-colored skin, round eyes and full lips. Traits that we'd inherited from our mother, Nona.

"Wow, you came home, huh?" Tennille said, brimming over with sarcasm.

"Yeah, it's good to see you," I said and then reached for Tennille in an attempt to hug her.

Tennille moved out of my reach, obviously rejecting my hug. "Uh, Mama's in the living room with Daddy. Who's this?" she asked, as she turned her attention to AJ.

I lowered my arms. "Uh, this is your nephew, AJ. AJ, you remember your Aunt Tennille?"

AJ shook his head. "Naw, but good to meet you, Aunt Tennille."

"Yeah, good to meet you, too. You are just like your daddy. I mean *just like him*. Where is the infamous Apollo, anyway?"

I dropped my eyes. "Um, he couldn't make it."

"Good," Tennille said. "Well, y'all come on in. Mommy and Daddy will be glad to see you."

AJ and I followed Tennille through the spacious foyer to the living room. I smiled as I entered the warmly decorated room to find my father sitting in his favorite recliner, my mother right by his side.

"Mommy, Daddy, Tonya's here," Tennille announced.

Rev. Thomas Langford's head snapped up, and he gave me a huge smile. "Tony!" he said, referring to me by a nickname I hadn't heard in years.

I walked over to my frail father and hugged him tightly with tears in my eyes. He was just a shell of the man he once was. Sickness had ravaged his body. He'd lost so much weight that he was nearly unrecognizable.

I leaned over and hugged my mother who wore a look of surprise on her face.

"Tony, I'm glad to see you, baby," my mother said. "Is this my grandson standing over here looking so handsome?"

I nodded and wiped a tear from my cheek. "Yes, ma'am. This is AJ."

"My Lord, he's grown! And he's the spitting image of his father. I haven't seen this boy in so long! The last time you were here you came alone."

"Yes ma'am. I sang at Daddy's church."

"Daddy's church? Christ Temple will always be your church, too," she replied and then turned her attention to AJ, "Boy, come on over here and hug your grandmother."

AJ smiled for the first time during the entire trip to Atlanta, then bent over and hugged my mother, then my father.

AJ and I sat on the sofa opposite my parents, and Tennille left the room.

"What brings you here, Tony? How long you staying?" my father asked.

"I just wanted to see y'all. AJ's on spring break this week, and I thought we'd spend the week here," I said.

"Where're your husband and Rebekah?" my mother interjected.

"Um, Apollo couldn't make it, and Rebekah's still at school. She'll be on spring break next week," I said. Well, I wasn't exactly lying. Apollo couldn't make it because he didn't even know I was there.

My mother nodded, but I sensed that she knew something was wrong.

"Well, let me show you two to your rooms. You can stay right down the hall from me and Daddy," she said as she stood from her chair. "TL, I'll be right back," she said to my father.

He coughed and nodded up at her. "Okay, Nona." He smiled at me and added, "It sure is good to see you, Tony."

I stood from the sofa and said, "It's even better to see you, Daddy."

AJ and I followed my mother through the spacious bungalow-style house and made our first stop at the room AJ would be sleeping in. He decided to lay down for a nap, and I followed my mother to the bedroom right next to his.

"Well, I guess it's a good thing you bought this house for us with all these bedrooms. At first I thought they'd go to waste, but since your daddy's been sick, we've needed the room for all the visitors," my mother said as she walked across the bedroom and opened the curtains.

I sat down on the side of the bed and gazed out the window. From that bedroom, I could see the luscious green backyard. I didn't even realize that I was crying until my mother mentioned it.

She walked over to the bed and sat down beside me. "What's wrong, Tony?"

I shook my head as I looked into eyes that were an older version of my own. "I didn't wanna bother you with this, but I couldn't think of anywhere else to go."

Concern filled my mother's eyes. "Well, what is it, baby? What's wrong? Are things okay between you and Apollo?"

My only reaction was to burst into tears. She'd hit the nail on the head—mother's instinct. My mother pulled me into her arms and rocked me as I cried. I buried my face in her shoulder, soaking up her comfort. It was exactly what I needed. My mother's comfort.

I cried until I ran out of tears, and then I lifted my head and wiped my face.

"Tell me what happened," she said softly.

I filled her in on everything that had happened from Lisa's visit, to AJ's arrest, to the revelation that Apollo had been cheating on me for years.

"Well, what are you gonna do?" she asked.

I shrugged. "I don't know. I love him, Mama. We've been together for so long. I don't know how to be without him. What would you do?"

"Well, I can tell you what I *did* do. I stayed, and I fought for my marriage."

I looked at her with confusion in my eyes. "You mean…"

She nodded. "Yes, your daddy cheated on me when you girls were small. It hurt, and I was angry. After all, I'd given up my career and changed my life to be with him." My mother had been a pretty successful soul singer before meeting and marrying my father.

"What did you do when you found out about him cheating?"

"I confronted him. Wacked him upside his head with a telephone and told him if it ever happened again, I'd take my girls and leave. Told him I'd find another husband and let him raise y'all. Well, he couldn't stand the thought of another man raising his girls. So he straightened up. It didn't hurt that I went over to that heifer's house and got her told, too."

I sighed. "Mama, the thing is, it's not just one woman. The way AJ tells it, there are several women, and he's been cheating for years. Ever since AJ and Beka were little. Plus, this Lisa girl says she's pregnant."

Mama nodded. "What does Apollo say?"

I shook my head. "Not much. Just denies everything."

"Tony, can I give you a little motherly advice?"

"Of course. That's why I'm here."

"Go back home to your husband. Tell him you forgive him and work things out with him."

With a furrowed brow, I said, "That's it? Forgive him for something he won't even admit to? How's that gonna work?"

"Look, baby. That's a good man, a preacher. You can't get any better than that. He stands right by your side and accepts your career. You're gone so much, you couldn't expect a man that good-looking not to be tempted to stray. Remember, the devil is always gonna try to attack him. Your job is to stand by his side. Go home, cut back on the travel, and fix your marriage. Don't just give that good man away."

"Mama, I just don't know. What about that girl and her baby?"

"Well, even if he did have sex with her, it doesn't mean it's his baby. Just call him. Y'all can work this out."

"Even if we *can* work things out, AJ's not gonna want to go home. He hates Apollo."

"Well, AJ can stay here. He's my grandchild, and we've got plenty of room. He's almost grown. You can't use him as an excuse to give up on your husband. Just think about it, Tony. I'll leave you and let you get some rest. Where's your luggage?"

I shook my head. "I was so upset, I didn't bring any."

Mama stood up and then leaned over and kissed me on the forehead. "Lord, have mercy. Girl, call your husband."

I watched as she left the room and wondered if things could be fixed. Could my marriage really be saved?

6

"Let Go"

THE NEXT MORNING I SAT IN THE WINDOW SEAT OF MY
temporary bedroom, distracted by the scene outside. My parents'
backyard was so lush and inviting that several squirrels had decided
to use it as a playground. I sat there with my Bible in my lap and
instead of reading the Word, I continued to stare out the window. It's
ironic how often I'd wondered about people's situations. *How did
they get into such a mess*, I'd ponder. Funny how quickly you can
find yourself in the midst of chaos. Trouble could come at anytime,
whether you were ready for it or not.

I hadn't called Apollo or answered his multiple calls. Instead, I
lay awake in bed most of the night, praying. I prayed for my family,
my marriage, peace, healing, direction, and strength. I'd found
comfort in my prayers and had felt God's presence envelope me. I'd
thanked Him and finally managed to get some sleep. I still awakened

early and decided to find more comfort in the Word. I looked down at the Bible and continued to read from Psalms chapter 3.

To the Lord I cry aloud, and he answers me from his holy hill. Selah.

I sighed and thought, *Lord, I know you hear me, but it still hurts.* I wiped a single tear as it rolled down my face and was startled by the buzzing of my cell phone. I checked the screen. It was Rebekah.

"Good morning," I said, trying to disguise the despair in my voice.

"Hey, Mama. You okay? AJ told me what happened," Rebekah replied. I could imagine that her wide-set eyes were full of sadness.

"I'm okay. Are *you* okay?" I replied. Rebekah adored her father. Hearing about his indiscretions had to have been hard for her.

"Well…yeah. I'm okay."

I rested my head on the cool glass of the window. "I was gonna tell you what happened. I was just trying to get my head together."

"Mama, I already knew."

I sat up straight and closed my Bible. "What? You already knew? How?"

"I found out two or three years ago. One of my friends told me."

"One of your friends?" *How many people know about this?* I felt like such a fool.

"Shayna. Daddy had been messing around with her mother. I'm sorry for not telling you, Mama."

I closed my Bible and shook my head. How had I been so blind? *The wife is always the last to know.* "No, baby. It wasn't your responsibility to tell me."

"Well, I kinda hate that you had to find out. Y'all were so happy."

"Yeah, baby. I thought so, too." I could feel the tears flooding my eyes. "I'll talk to you, later, Beka. Okay?"

"Yes, ma'am. I love you, Mama."

"I love you, too."

I laid my phone down and began another cycle of sobs and prayer.

♪♪♪

It was my third day in Atlanta. I sat in a chair in my parents' bedroom and watched as the Hospice nurse checked my father's vital signs. He seemed to grow weaker and weaker as the hours passed, and it was increasingly difficult for me to retain my tears when I was around him. The thought of losing my marriage was painful, but the thought of losing my father was just unbearable. As I sat there, I closed my eyes and prayed.

Father God, please touch my father. Lord, in accordance with Your Word, I pray that you raise him up. Lord, strengthen my mother both physically and spiritually. And Lord, strengthen my sisters. Finally Lord, strengthen me. In Jesus' name. Amen.

I opened my eyes and found that I was now in the room alone with Daddy.

He smiled. "Were you praying for me, Tony?"

I offered him a weak smile. "Yes, sir."

"I thank you. If anyone can get a prayer through, I know you can."

I stood and walked over to the bed. I sat down beside him and grasped his hand. His lips were so dry, so I reached for the cup of water on the night table. He shook his head and pushed it away.

"Fluid restrictions. My kidneys are gone. All those years, I refused to eat right. This high blood pressure and diabetes is gon' be the death of me," he said.

"Daddy, don't say that. God can heal you. Nothing's too hard for him."

He reached up and rubbed my cheek. "Tony, I have accepted God's will, and I'm not afraid. I'm glad you came. I'm glad you'll be here to see me off."

I felt the warm tears as they trickled down my cheeks. My father handed me a tissue from the box that sat beside him on the bed.

"Tony, I need to tell you something."

I looked at him through my fuzzy eyes. "Yes, sir?"

"You can't run from your problems. I'm glad you're here, but I know why you left home."

"Mama told you?"

"She didn't have to. I'm sick—not blind. I could see it all over you the day you got here. I could see it in your countenance."

I shut my eyes and shook my head. "Daddy, I don't know what to do. Mama says to just go home and forgive him, but I can't see how

.things could be that simple. I've prayed and prayed, and I'm still so confused. I can't understand why this happened to me and to you. We've devoted our lives to doing God's work."

"Baby girl, an untested faith is an unreliable faith. Sometimes we experience trials to bring us closer to God, to give our witness, our testimony, new power."

I nodded. "I know you're right. It's just so hard."

"I know you want me to tell you what to do, but I can't do that. Besides, you already know."

"I do?"

He nodded. "You know the Word. The Holy Spirit will lead you, but you've got to let Him. You can't let your emotions get in the way, and you can't look for someone to give you the answer. This is between you and your husband and God."

I nodded. He was right. I could pray all day long, but if I was gonna let my emotions or someone else's opinion rule me, I'd never make any progress. I leaned over and hugged him. He kissed my cheek and rubbed my back.

"I love you, Tony."

I smiled down at him and inspected his face as if trying to commit it to memory. His strong jaw was now slack, his chiseled features sagged. His small eyes, once full of life, were weak. But to me, Thomas Lawrence Langford was still the handsomest man in the entire world.

"I love you, too, Daddy."

"Will you sing me a song, Tony? I need to hear that beautiful voice."

I nodded again and sucked in a deep breath. "Anything for you."

I closed my eyes and began to sing my father's favorite song, "Amazing Grace." I held his hand and serenaded him until he drifted off to sleep. I kissed his forehead and looked up to see both Tennille and my mother standing in the doorway with tears in their eyes. I hugged them both and then stepped out into the hallway. My father passed away early the next morning.

7

"I'll Make It"

I STOOD BEFORE MY FATHER'S CASKET AND WISHED THAT I was in the middle of a bad dream. It would have been a relief to wake up and find that instead of listening to other preachers speak about my father, I'd be able to walk into his study and see him working on his sermon as he did every Saturday morning. Instead, I was standing at his grave site, tears flowing from my eyes as the sun shone brightly, its rays warming my face. Apollo, who stood next to me, reached over and grasped my hand. I didn't resist. I needed to feel a human touch, even if it was *his* touch.

I glanced around me. To my left stood my mother and my three sisters, all in tears. On the other side of Apollo stood AJ, who'd promised to behave himself for his Pop-Pop's funeral. I released a ragged sigh as they began to lower my father's casket into the ground. Theresa, my oldest sister, let out a loud wail as they lowered the coffin. Her husband, Greg, wrapped his arms around her and pulled her close to him as her two adult children hovered over her. Toi and Tennille held onto either side of Mama as if holding her up on her feet. I felt Rebekah rest her hand on my shoulder. I turned around and smiled weakly at her through my tears.

As we walked from the grave site to the limo, Apollo lifted my hand and kissed it. I leaned against him and laid my head on his shoulder.

Back at my parents' house, I sat alone in the den while the other family members crowded into the kitchen, fixing plates and chatting with one another. I looked up and smiled as Apollo walked towards me with a plate in one hand and a canned soda in the other.

"Is that for me?" I asked.

"Yes, ma'am. You need to eat."

I took the plate, sat it in my lap, and stared down at it.

"Tonya, eat something."

I picked up the fork and moved the food around on the plate.

Apollo sighed. "Would you feel better if you went in the kitchen and ate with your family?"

I shook my head. "Not really. I'm still an outcast, you know."

"No one's gonna start with you on a day like this. They can't still be bitter about the break-up of the group."

I stared down at the plate. "Neither of them has said as much as two words to me."

"And you think it's because of something that happened more than twenty years ago? That's crazy."

I looked at him out of the corner of my eye. "You'd be surprised at how long the women in my family can hold a grudge."

Apollo cleared his throat and shifted his body on the sofa beside me. He'd obviously caught the double meaning in my statement. "Well, no matter where you're gonna sit, you need to eat." He sat there a few seconds and then quietly asked, "Are you coming home with me?"

I shrugged. "I don't know yet. Maybe I should stay here with my mom. Maybe she needs me here."

"You can stay here with your mother for as long as you need to. I just need to know if you're eventually coming home."

I looked him directly in the eye. "Why should I? What's changed?"

"You're my wife, Tonya, and I didn't think that you took those vows so lightly."

I was shocked. "*Me* take them lightly? *Really?*"

"Look, I don't want to argue with you. I love you, Tonya. And I need you. I'm asking you to come back home. *Please.*"

I saw the sincerity in his eyes. I *had* taken vows. Didn't that mean that I had to at least *try* to save my marriage? I sighed. I turned my head and saw my sister, Toi, standing in the doorway, glaring at me. That sealed my decision. "I guess I will," I said. I obviously wasn't welcome there.

Apollo relaxed his posture. "Okay, good. When?"

"I'll go pack right now."

♪♪♪

I leaned over the bed and piled the clothes I'd purchased during my visit into my new suitcase. I was more than apprehensive about returning home. There were still so many unresolved issues between me and Apollo and between Apollo and A.J. But we'd been married for more than half of my life. I knew I had to try to make it work. Try was all I could do.

 I turned and headed to the bathroom to retrieve my toiletries. It was then that I noticed Tennille standing in the hall outside the room.

"Hey," she said. "You leaving so soon?"

I stopped dead in my tracks. She almost sounded cordial."Uh, yeah. I told Mama already."

"Yeah, she told me."

We endured a moment of silence, and then she said, "You don't have to go, I mean, if you don't want to. You can stay for as long as you need to."

I smiled. "Thank you, Tennille. It means a lot to hear you say that, but I need to go. I've got a lot to work on."

She nodded. "Apollo."

"Yeah, Apollo, my marriage, my family."

"I don't like him. Never have. But if you want things to work out, then I hope they do."

I walked over to her and hugged her. "Thank you."

"You can call me. You know, if you wanna talk or something."

"I'd like that. I've missed you. I've missed all of my sisters."

She smiled. "Yeah, well, Theresa and Toi will come around, too."

I hoisted the suitcase up off of the bed as Apollo walked past Tennille and into the room.

"I hope so," I said. "Bye, Tennille."

"Bye, Tony."

♪♪♪

I was back home, in my own bed, lying next to my husband. I scooted closer to the edge of the bed and felt Apollo tighten his grip on me. He'd been this way since I'd returned home a few weeks earlier. Considerate, attentive, and loving; all the things a wife desired in a husband. The thing is, Apollo was *always* loving and attentive when I was home. Still, things just didn't feel exactly right. I didn't feel for him the way I felt before AJ's revelation. I'd lost that intense adoration I'd always felt for him. My total respect and trust for him was gone. I loved him, but not like I once had.

In the weeks since my return home, we celebrated AJ's high school graduation. He'd moved in with one of his friends shortly thereafter. He and Apollo were on speaking terms, but nothing more. Rebekah had accepted a summer internship and only spent a few days at home after finishing the spring semester of college. That only left me and Apollo in that big house. Alone to face what was left of our marriage, and alone to try and salvage it.

Apollo had yet to even acknowledge his indiscretions, let alone apologize for them. Gwen Donley abruptly resigned from her position at the church, and neither she nor her daughter had been to worship service in weeks. The position of church secretary was now held by Sister Rena Jones, a rather plain and mousy young lady who was too young to have a daughter for Apollo to hit on. I suspected that Apollo had hand-picked her, believing that I wouldn't see her as a threat.

I squeezed my eyes shut in an attempt to attract sleep. But I was wide awake, just as I had been most nights since my return home. I hadn't performed or spoken at any events. I spent most of my time at home, cooking and playing house with Apollo, and I'm sorry to say, it wasn't working. I finally pried Apollo's arm from around my waist and sat up on the side of the bed.

"Where you going?" he asked groggily.

"To pray," I said as I stood from the bed and tied the belt on my robe.

"Ok, hurry back." *You'd think he'd want to pray with me.*

I walked down the hall to the guest bedroom and kneeled by the bed.

Heavenly Father, I need you now. I need you to lead and guide me. Show me what to do. Should I stay in this marriage? Has my husband changed? Lord, I'm lost. I need your help. Help me please…help me please…

8

"Up Above My Head"

"HE'S STILL IN THE MEETING," RENA SAID.

I sighed. He'd been in that meeting for at least two hours. I knew he was supposed to meet with the trustees but this was especially long-winded, even for them. I laid my phone down and stared across the living room at the clock—12:45. We were supposed to meet for lunch and I was getting pretty hungry. I sat there for a few more minutes and then grabbed my keys and left. I was sure that when he saw me, he'd be more than willing to shut that meeting down.

I made the short drive to the church and parked my car next to Apollo's. I stepped out of my car and glanced around the parking lot. There were only a couple of cars there other than mine and Apollo's. *Hmm, I guess they finally finished with meeting. I'm right on time.*

I entered the church annex through the glass double doors and headed straight to Apollo's office. I breezed by Rena's desk and threw her a quick "hello" before attempting to open the door to Apollo's office. It was locked. I turned and looked at Rena.

Reading my expression, she said, "He's still in the meeting."

I frowned. "With who?" Unless the trustees had all ridden in the same car, he definitely wasn't in any meeting with them.

She shrugged. "One of the members? I'm not sure what her name is. This membership is so large."

I nodded and took a seat in one of the chairs lining the wall of the outer office. I sat there for at least ten full minutes and was beginning to get a little irritated. Apollo knew we were having lunch together. *He* had suggested it. The least he could do was to let me know he was running late. I tapped my foot on the floor and thumbed through a Christian magazine. I looked up at Rena, who looked a little irritated herself.

"Have you had lunch, Rena?" I asked.

"Well, no ma'am. Pastor Hill said he was not to be disturbed, and I didn't want to interrupt him to let him know I was going to lunch, so I've just been waiting."

I stood and walked over to her desk. "Why don't you go ahead? I'll man the desk until you get back."

Her eyes lit up. "Are you sure? I mean, is that permitted?"

I smiled. "Honey, I'm the first lady. I think it'll be okay."

She laughed nervously. "Okay, well, thanks, Mrs. Hill."

"No problem."

I took her seat behind the mahogany desk and continued to wait.

Whatever they were discussing must have been pretty deep, because it sure was taking long enough. I don't know who or what it was, but something told me to walk over by the door to Apollo's office and try to sneak a listen at their conversation. Well, that's not entirely true. I think we both know who told me to do that, and it wasn't God.

I walked over to the glass doors and checked to see that Rena had left the parking lot and that no one else had arrived. Certain that the coast was clear, I locked them and crept back to the wooden door that led to Apollo's office. I pressed my ear against it and closed my eyes. *Lord, is this what my marriage has come to?* I shook my head in disgust, but continued to listen.

"You gotta be patient. Things have to be this way until I can figure something else out." That was Apollo.

"Patient? Patient? I've *been* patient, Apollo!" That was Ms. What's-her-name, and she sounded upset.

"I know you have, baby. But you got to understand that this situation is very delicate. I stand to lose a lot." *Baby?* I started to knock on the door and break this thing up, but I couldn't. I wanted and needed to hear more.

"Yeah, well I'm tired, Apollo. You say you love me. You say you gon' leave her. Then leave her!" My eyes stretched wide. *What?*

"Kay, look. You know I love you, but I can't leave her right now. I'll lose the church. Plus, you can't just up and leave your husband. There's a lot we have to consider." Kay? Kay Smith? She was the wife of one of our newer deacons.

"Well, you can consider this. You won't be getting no more of this until you make a move. No more late night phone calls, no more lunch meetings in your office, no more nothing with me! You hear me?!" She was shouting now.

"Calm down. Give me some time. You know it's you I want. Look, being married to Tonya is just a front. My marriage has been over for years now. We'll be together. I promise. Now, come here."

I backed away from the door, my ears ringing from what I'd just heard. I stormed out of the office and right past Rena, who'd made it back from lunch. I made a beeline to my house, parked in my driveway, slammed my car door shut, entered the house, and kicked my black pumps off by the front door. I rolled up the sleeves on my pink sweater and took the stairs two-at-a-time, quickly reaching the second floor. I walked into my bedroom, headed straight to the closet, grabbed the suitcases, and began to pack. The adrenaline from my anger took over and before I knew it, I was done.

One after the other, I dragged the luggage down the stairs, through the front door, and to the curb next to my driveway. On my fifth trip, one of my neighbors, Mrs. Dendy, met me at the curb.

"You setting up for a yard sale, Tonya?"

I looked up at her and wiped the sweat from my brow. "No, I'm actually giving this stuff away. Feel free to look through it."

"Oh, okay."

I turned and walked back inside my house in time to answer the ringing phone.

"Hello?"

"Hey, Rena told me you came by. I'm sorry about lunch. I got tied up." *I bet you did.*

"I see." I sounded pretty emotionless. It was the only way I could keep from crying or screaming into the phone.

He cleared his throat. "Um, well, we could go out for dinner if you want. Let me make it up to you."

"That's alright. I think I'd like to stay in for dinner tonight."

"Ok, whatever you want."

"Okay, well, see you at dinner then."

"Okay. Love you."

I gritted my teeth and squeezed my eyes shut as I said, "Love you, too."

I hung up and headed to the kitchen where I took my time and prepared a dinner of t-bone steaks, baked potatoes, and Caesar salad. I set the table and sat in the living room with a glass of wine while I waited for Apollo's arrival.

At around 6:45 P.M., I heard Apollo pull his car into the driveway. Leaving my post in the living room, I placed the food on the dining room table and lit the tapered candle that stood in the middle. I pulled Apollo's chair out, then sat in my chair at the opposite end of the table.

Apollo walked in the door and said, "Baby, I'm home."

I closed my eyes and told myself to calm down. The sound of him calling me baby almost sent me into a rage. "In here," I said, calmly.

Apollo walked into the dining room with a bouquet of yellow roses in his hand—my favorite. He leaned over and kissed me on the cheek. I forced a smile as I took the flowers from him.

"Thank you."

"Anything for my lovely wife. Dinner looks great. Let me go and wash my hands."

I nodded. "Okay."

A few seconds later, Apollo led us in grace, and we began to eat our dinner. He chattered on about his fabricated meeting with the church trustees, and I listened to his lies as if I believed them. I smiled and played the role of the happy wife pretty well. Maybe we *were* a good match. After all, he'd been pretending to be a loving husband for God knows how long.

I served Apollo a piece of store-bought apple pie for desert and watched as he shoveled it into his mouth. In the back of my mind, I wished the pie was laced with poison. *Lord, forgive me.*

"So, no Tonya for dessert tonight?" he asked between bites.

"Is that what you want? You want some Tonya for dessert?" I asked evenly.

He smiled at me. "I always want some Tonya for dessert. I want some Tonya for every meal."

I nodded. "Meet me upstairs when you're done with your pie."

I stood and left the table without another word.

9

"Shackles"

I LAY IN THE BED WITH MY EYES WIDE OPEN, STARING AT the ceiling. Apollo was planting kisses all over my body, and I felt dirty, filthy. I let him kiss and caress me until I thought I'd die. When I could take no more, I shoved Apollo away and sat up on the side of the bed. He reached for me. I snatched away.

"What's wrong?" he asked.

I sighed. "I think this has gone far enough. I can't take anymore. You need to leave now."

Apollo frowned. "What? You got me all hot and ready...you can't leave me hanging like this! Tonya, what's going on?"

I stood from the bed and wrapped my robe around my body. "I overheard your little tiff with Kay this afternoon and it's now clear to me what your true feelings are."

Apollo stood from the bed naked as a jaybird, a look of disbelief on his face. "You were eavesdropping *again*? Come on, Tonya. That's beneath you."

I shook my head. "You're not gonna do this again. You're not gonna skirt your way around this. It's not about me eavesdropping. It's about what I heard."

With a smug look on his face, he said, "How you know that was me? Did you see me?"

I have never wanted to slap a person so badly in all my life. "I think I know the voice of the man I've been married to for more than *twenty years*! I cannot believe you! I *know* it was you."

"Well, it's not what you think. We were—"

I held up my hand. "Unh uh. No sir. This time I want you to do something that's rare for you. I want you to be a man. Be a man, and tell the truth. Let me keep the shred of respect I have left for you."

He frowned. "Whatchu mean, 'be a man'? I've been the man you love for more than twenty years. Are you seriously trying to put me out over what you *think* you've heard?"

I shook my head and threw up my hands. "Why would I think a man who's been lying to me for years would tell me the truth *now*? Just go, Apollo. Go to Kay or Lisa or whoever you want. Just leave. I'm tired of living a lie, and I'm tired of *you*."

He sat down on the bed and dropped his head. "Okay, I'm sorry."

I folded my arms across my chest. "For what?"

He looked up at me with what could almost pass as remorse in his eyes. "Come on, Tonya. I'm trying to apologize. Isn't this what you wanted?"

"What are you apologizing for, Apollo?"

"I cheated on you. I'm sorry."

I was quiet for a moment. I couldn't believe that he was actually admitting to his infidelity. "With who, Kay?" I finally asked.

He nodded. "Yeah, but she didn't mean anything to me. You were gone so much. I was lonely, and I just needed someone."

I stared at the floor. "Who else?"

"Huh?"

"Who else? Lisa?"

"Tonya, I—"

"Who else?!" I screamed. "You were man enough to do it. You should be man enough to confess!" I wanted the whole truth, even if it killed me to hear it and right at that moment, I actually felt like a part of me was dying.

"Okay, okay. Yeah, Lisa, too."

"Her baby yours?"

He shook his head. "I don't know," he groaned.

"Are there more women?"

"Yes."

"A lot?"

He sighed. "Yes."

I sat down next to him on the bed and shook my head in disgust.

"I'm sorry, Tonya. I love you."

I nodded slowly. "Humph. So you say."

"But I do. *I really do.* I don't know why I cheated. Maybe I'm a sex addict. I'll get help, some counseling. It'll never happen again."

"I know it won't." I turned and looked him straight in the eye. "Here's what we're gonna do. You're gonna leave now. You're gonna leave, and you're gonna go to Lisa or Kay or whoever, and you're gonna do whatever you want to do. But you're gonna leave this house, and you're never coming back."

He gave me a startled look. "Tonya—"

"No, this is over. You don't love me, and I doubt if you ever did. I'm done with you, with this sham of a marriage."

"Come on, now. We can work this out."

"No, we can't. Remember, I *heard* you today. I didn't get this information second-hand or from the rumor mill. I *heard* about how our marriage is just a front, and the only reason you're still here is because you stand to lose so much. I *HEARD* IT! But I never once *heard* you say that *I* was one of the things you didn't want to lose."

"Come on, Tonya. I *had* to say those things to her. I had to calm her down so she wouldn't go running off at the mouth. We don't need that kind of publicity."

"We? *We?* So, *now* it's we? No, I think the only person you're concerned about is *you. You* don't wanna lose your status or your megachurch. *You're* holding onto this marriage because of my fame—not my love. It's over. I've tried, and I've failed to keep this marriage together."

I stood and gathered the clothes he'd shed from the chair in the corner of the room. "Get dressed, and go."

"Tonya—"

I felt my head begin to ache. "Go! Leave before I call the police and have you put out of here!"

He stood up and snatched his clothes from me. "The police can't put me out of my own house, Tonya. You don't have grounds for it."

I stepped so close to him that I could feel his breath against my face as I looked up at him. I raised my eyebrows. "I'm not above saying that you hit me."

"So, now you're a liar? The Anointed Woman of God is a liar?" He scoffed as he pulled his underwear on.

"If the 'Mighty Man of God' can cheat, I guess I can lie," I shot back. "Besides, you'll probably want to hit me since I gave all of your clothes away."

He stopped in the middle of buttoning up his shirt and looked at me. "What did you say?"

"I *said* that I gave all of your stuff away—*all of it*. I put it out on the curb, and the neighbors had a good time looking through it. I even threw in your Gucci luggage for good measure. I was gonna throw those clothes away too and send you out of here naked, but I just couldn't go through with the sex. You disgust me."

The look in his eyes told me that he *did* want to hit me. He clenched his fists and glared at me. His nostrils flared.

I smiled. "Go ahead, Apollo. Hit me if you wanna hit me. You've disrespected me in all other ways possible, made a fool of me, lied to me, and terrorized my children into keeping your secrets. So go ahead and put the icing on the cake. Show me how you *really* feel about me, about our marriage."

He stood there for a moment and then started laughing. His laughter sent a chill down my spine. It was full off icy disdain. He draped his tie around his neck and shook his head. Then he tossed me a look that said, *you poor pathetic thing.* "You know what? You're stupid. You are a stupid, silly woman. I am so damn tired of you! I'm *glad* to be rid of your big butt. You're boring—no life in you. You're insecure, and you're just plain dumb. Yeah, I married you for your name *and* your fame, and it worked. But I just can't take any more of you. I'm glad it's over because you make me sick! Plus, you're bad in bed. I *had* to cheat on you just to get some real satisfaction. You're *lucky* I married you. I can get another you any day, but you will *never* find another me!"

I have to admit that I was more than taken aback. So this is what he really thought of me after all these years? Two children, twenty plus years, and it was a sham from the start? I think I must've blacked out or something because all I can remember after that is picking the lamp up from the bedside table. Hours later, the police arrived to take my statement, but I couldn't give them one. They told me that I'd given Apollo a concussion...that I'd hit him in the head with the lamp and knocked him out cold. They said I called 911. They arrested me, said that he might press charges. I didn't care. I was tired. I was hurt. I was done.

10

"No, Never"

I WAS SITTING IN THE SUNROOM AT THE REAR OF MY
house. My Bible sat open in my lap. I traced my finger along the
passage and mouthed the words. I closed my eyes and sighed. It had
been six months since I put Apollo out of the house. Six months, and
I still couldn't concentrate on the Word. Six months, and my prayers
seemed so empty. Six months, and I hadn't sung even one song of
praise. Six months, and the blood that ran through my veins still ran
cold. Six months, and I still hated Rev. Apollo David Hill, Sr. I was
beginning to wonder if I'd ever heal.

The phone rang, and I was tempted not to answer it. I didn't want
to talk to anyone. I didn't want to do anything, but I answered it
anyway.

"Hello."

"Ms. Tonya? Palmer Criss, here. Thank God, I finally reached you. Did you get my messages?" Palmer was my manager, and yes, I'd received his messages, but I didn't want to talk to anyone— including him.

"Yes, I did," was my slow answer.

"Well, then you know that we're due back in the studio next week."

I shook my head. "I'm not ready to record, Palmer. Have you forgotten the little fact that my divorce was just finalized or that I lost my dad less than a year ago?"

"I understand, but maybe it'll be therapeutic for you to get back to work. Plus, the company is really laying on the pressure. They want a finished product by the summer. They've already lined up some great producers for you."

I sighed. "Well, why don't *they* get together and record an album, then."

"Look, Tonya. I know you're in a bad place right now, but you don't wanna mess things up with your record company. You're under contractual obligation to record one more album."

I shut my Bible and laid it on the wicker end table. "Fine. Where are we recording? Atlanta?" I hoped so. At least then I'd get to visit my mother and Tennille. We'd grown a lot closer during my divorce.

"Well, that's the exciting part. We've got a new producer who's come on board. You'll be travelling to his studio to record."

I was less than enthused. "Well, who is it? Where am I going?"

"It's Kwame Kane! He's created several tracks for you. He's

really excited about working with you."

"Kwame Kane? You mean, Kwame 'The Swami' Kane? Doesn't he produce Hip Hop or gangster rap or something?"

"So, you know of him?"

"Well, yeah. I think I've heard my son talk about him or maybe I saw a couple of his videos. Look, Palmer. I sing gospel. *Traditional* gospel. I'm not trying to change my sound."

"The guy is a genius! The label thinks working with Kwame could bring you crossover success. They're really adamant about Kwame working on this album."

I shook my head. "I don't like this. I don't like it at all. I'm Shirley Caesar, *not* Kirk Franklin."

"Okay, I hear you. But think of the new people you can reach with a new sound. It's all about glorifying God and bringing souls to Christ, right?"

How could I argue with that? "Yeah, it is. Okay...okay, I'll work with him, but why do I feel like I just sold my soul to the devil?"

Palmer laughed. "You didn't, I promise. His studio's in Virginia. I'll send you the travel information."

♪♪♪

"I can't believe they're forcing me into working with this guy," I said, my tone laced with disgust.

"Well, is his reputation *that* bad? You make it sound like

punishment," Tennille asked.

I shrugged as if she could see me through the phone. "I don't know about his reputation, but I've been watching his videos on the internet. He's always jumping and hopping around like a fool. Always got a neck full of gold and a mouth full of diamonds, and he dresses like a clown."

Tennille laughed. "Wow, I'ma have to check some of those videos out. Sounds entertaining."

"It's stupid, and he *looks* stupid. He better not even think about jumping around in a video with me. That is not happening!"

Tennille laughed again. "What about the music? Is it any good?"

"I guess. I couldn't really tell, though. You know I'm not into rap."

"So, what are you gonna do? Are you gonna work with him?"

"I don't really have a choice. I can't afford to breach my contract, especially since Apollo already took me to the cleaners."

"Yeah, well, I still say you should've fought him to the death. He didn't deserve a dime."

"I know. Anyway, let me get off and go pack. Tell Mama I'll call her later. Is she doing alright?"

"She's better and better every day. I'll be praying that all goes well with you and Mr. Kane."

"Please do. I need all the prayer I can get."

♪♪♪

I stepped out of the car and walked up to the white-washed stone building. Etched into the glass entry door was an illustration of Kwame Kane, sitting Indian-style with his eyes closed. His hands were clasped in front of him. He wore an Arabian tunic and a turban. Underneath the logo were the words, "Swami Productions". I rolled my eyes and thought, *so this man is gonna produce a gospel album, huh?*

I followed a young intern through the building to a small waiting area. He assured me that Mr. Kane would be right with me and then left me to wait alone. I sat on a sofa and took in my surroundings: plush white carpet, old Hollywood-style white cloth couches and chairs, mirrored tables, platinum and gold album plaques, and framed magazine covers lining the walls. It wasn't flashy or gaudy as I'd expected. On the contrary, it was rather elegant.

I sat there for a few moments and then picked up a magazine and began to thumb through it. I sat there long enough to read through three magazines, check my messages and emails on my phone and use the restroom *twice*. I was fast losing my patience with Mr. Kwame Kane. After all, it was *him* who wanted to work with *me*. I pulled out my phone and dialed Palmer's number.

"Tonya! How's it going?"

"Well, it's going *great* if the company wanted me to be able to describe Mr. Kane's lobby in detail."

"What do you mean?"

"I mean that this guy is so darned busy that he had an intern greet me and stash me in his lobby. I've been here for hours, and I've *yet* to meet him. You can just tell A&R or whoever else at the label that I don't care how they feel about this guy, I'm not gonna sit here and be treated like this!" I was into a full-on rant.

"Okay, okay, calm down. Let me check into this."

"Yeah, you *better* check into this. I flew all the way here, to some little fishy-smelling town that I didn't even know existed, and for what? To sit in the lobby like I'm on an audition? I already have a record deal, or doesn't *Mr. Kwame 'The Swami' Kane* know this? I'm not some young desperate girl willing to take any and everything for a shot. *I'm* a legend. I have earned some respect!" I could feel my temper and the volume of my voice rising.

"Tonya, just take it easy and let me check on this."

"Take it easy? How can—" I was interrupted by a tap on my shoulder. I spun around with a frown and was face to face with none other than Mr. Kwame Kane.

"Never mind, here he is," I hissed into the phone and then ended the call. I eyed the man who only stood a couple of inches taller than my 5'5" and shoved my cell phone into the hip pocket of my jeans.

"Mrs. Hill?" he asked.

"It's *Ms.* Langford," I answered, curtly. I adjusted my purse strap on my shoulder and folded my arms across my chest.

"Oh, sorry about that. Are you ready to get to work?" He was acting like I hadn't been waiting for him for half a darn day.

"Mr. Kane, I presume?"

He smiled, revealing a mouth full of braces. *Ew. What grown man wears braces?* "Um, yes, I am," he said.

"Well, *Mr. Kane*, I've been out here ready to work for a while now. I don't know what you might have heard about me, and I don't know what kind of people you're used to dealing with, but I'm a professional, and I've been in this business for a long time. I don't appreciate being ushered into a room by some intern and left in the lurch like this."

He raised his eyebrows. "Um, I was really busy, but I'm ready now if you are."

The more upset I got, the calmer he seemed to get, which served to fuel my anger. "*Busy?* I flew all the way from my home, halfway across the country, and you *knew* I was coming, and all you can say is that you were *busy?*"

He sighed. *Oh, so I guess I'm getting on his nerves now.*

"Mrs. Hi—I mean, *Ms.* Langford, I apologize. I will be more sensitive to your time in the future. I'm really excited about working with you, so, can we begin?"

I glared at him for a moment. I had a mind to turn around, walk back out the front doors, and head back to Arkansas on the first thing smoking. But I didn't. Instead, I followed him into the soundproof studio.

I inspected him from the corner of my eye as he spoke with Fred, the engineer. Kwame was an okay-looking guy, but nothing to write home about. He had a medium build and smooth dark chocolate skin. He'd do, but he couldn't compete with Apollo. Wait, why was I comparing him to Apollo? I shook my head. I must have been losing it to be bringing up Apollo, even if it was just in my mind.

"Get it together, Tonya," I whispered to myself.

Kwame looked up at me. "What was that?" he asked.

"Oh…uh, nothing" I said.

"Okay, well, I was telling Fred, here, that I wanna start with a slow track. One of my staff writers wrote some awesome lyrics. I thought we could lay down a little something today and build on it."

I shrugged. "Okay. What's it called?"

"No title yet." He handed me the lyric sheet. "Oh, and welcome to the lab." *Yeah, whatever.*

About thirty minutes later, I was in the recording booth, listening to the track's intro. At Kwame's signal, I began to sing the lyrics. After singing a couple of lines, I snatched the headphones off of my head.

"I can't hear myself in *either ear*," I said, my frustration growing by the second. "And can someone get me a water with lemon, no ice?" *Rudeness, shotty equipment, what next?*

Kwame nodded and spoke into the intercom. "Um, okay. Let me check on the sound. We'll get your water, too."

A few moments later, I began singing again. This time I was able to hear myself.

"Lord, you know me

You've seen the troubles that have come
Lord, you love me
Despite the things that I've done
Lord, you hold me,
In the palm of your hand
You've even numbered the many hairs on my head

Every single strand

So awesome you are to me
So precious your grace and mercy
But, Lord, I have to ask, why me? Why me…"

I continued to sing through the entire track without even one interruption from Mr. Kane. Once I was finished, I looked up to see Kwame and the engineer applauding.

Kwame leaned close to the intercom and said, "That is why I wanted to work with you. *That* was incredible."

I smiled despite myself. "Why don't we call it, 'Why Me'?"

Kwame returned my smile. "Perfect."

11

"Go Through"

I'D SETTLED INTO THE BED IN MY SUITE, AND BEFORE I could close my eyes good, I heard a knock at the door. I groaned. It had been a long, but productive day in the studio, and all I could think about was getting some rest. Kwame was nothing if not a perfectionist, and he'd proven that during our first session.

I sat up on the side of the bed, pulled on my robe, and walked to the door. "Who is it?"

"Wesley, Mr. Kane's assistant."

I opened the door to find the young man whom I had assumed was an intern standing there holding a huge fruit basket.

"Oh, can I help you?" I asked.

He handed me the fruit basket, a bouquet of pale pink roses, and a card. "From Mr. Kane," he said.

I nodded and thanked him with a smile. I closed the door, set my gifts down, and then tore into the card. It read:

My apologies for inconveniencing you today. I look forward to our continued collaboration. Kwame.

At that point, I didn't know what to think. Mr. Kane was proving to be the polar opposite of what I had expected of him. I had to admit that he was wildly talented, and I was actually looking forward to the next day in the studio. What magic would Kwame and I manage to work together?

The next day, I was led straight into the studio—no waiting. I nodded a greeting at Fred and Kwame, who looked up from the sound board for a moment, smiled at me, and then continued his conversation with a young lady whom I'd later find out was one of his lyricists. Once they were finished talking, she left and he turned his attention to me.

"You get a good night's sleep?" he asked.

I smiled. "Yeah, I did."

"Good, we've got a long day ahead of us."

"Okay. Um, thanks for the gifts."

His smiled again. "Oh good, you got them. It was the least I could do. I'm really sorry about yesterday."

I felt more than a little sheepish. "Well, thanks."

He clapped his hands together. The silver ring he wore on his thumb gleamed against the lights in the room. "Alright, let's get to it. I wanted to ask you, do you write songs? I mean, do you have anything you'd like to work on?"

The truth was that I'd written many songs in my lifetime, most of which became hits. But I hadn't been able to write even one word since my separation. I was too ashamed to admit this, so I just said, "No."

"Okay, well here we go. I've got an upbeat track I created last night after you left. I want you to listen to it and see if you can come up with some lyrics."

My eyes widened. "You stayed here and made another track last night?"

He nodded. "Yeah, I was inspired by our session. I got this beat in my head and I had to go ahead and lay the track down. I was here until like three this morning."

I stared at him for a moment. That was just five hours ago. "You don't even look tired. How long did you get to sleep?"

He shrugged. "Oh, a couple of hours. I'm used to it."

I nodded slowly. "Right. If you say so."

He laughed. "No, seriously, I am."

He played the track for me. It had a little reggae flavor to it. It was definitely something that would get people up and on their feet. I prayed that God would give me the words to go along with the track. I really wanted to record the song.

I spent that day mostly listening to the many tracks that Kwame had created for my album. Honestly, they were all incredible and he'd created enough of them for two or three albums. I watched his face light up as he nodded his head or tapped his feet to the music. It was obvious that he loved what he did for a living. I hated to admit it, but I was enjoying working with Mr. Kwame Kane, and I hadn't ruled out working with him on future projects.

♪♪♪

I sat at the small table in my room, pushing my food around on my plate as I listened to Rebekah chatter on. I smiled as she discussed her classes. She was majoring in Political Science and planned to attend Law School. There was no doubt that she would easily achieve all of her goals. She was a very smart girl.

"So, how are things going there with the infamous Mr. Kane?" she asked.

I laughed. "Actually, I'm beginning to think that I misjudged him. He's really quiet and polite."

"Really? I wouldn't have guessed that."

"Me either. I guess I should've known better, though. I'm supposed to a Christian. Prejudging people is supposed to be a no-no for me. I'm just a mess right now, but you don't need to hear this."

"Mama, I'm not a baby. I know you've been through a lot lately. You're just off-balance."

That was an understatement. I cleared my throat, and said, "Have you spoken to your father lately?" I don't even know why I asked about him. He hadn't said two words to me since I put him out. No apology for the things he'd said. He'd only agreed to drop the assault charges against me in exchange for a huge divorce settlement. He obviously didn't care, so why did I?

"Um, yeah," was her only response but I could hear in her voice that there was more to that statement.

"What is it, Beka?"

"I'm only telling you this because I don't think it would be right for you to find out from someone else."

"Find out what?"

"Daddy and Lisa Donley got married last week."

I almost dropped the phone. "What?"

"Yeah, he called and told me a couple of days ago."

"B…but our divorce has only been final for a couple of months. He's already *married*?"

"Yeah, and he's starting a new church. Some of his old members are following him." That was no surprise. A lot of the members were very loyal to him. They had fiercely protested when the church forced him to resign, but once I filed for divorce, women came out of the woodwork, confessing to having had affairs with Apollo. The trustees had no choice but to let him go.

I held the phone for a moment. I would be lying if I said I wasn't upset. Had our marriage been so disposable to him that he could up and marry another woman in such a short amount of time? Evidently so.

"Um, I'll talk to you tomorrow, sweetie. I'm kinda tired."

Rebekah could surely hear the distress in my voice. "Mama, I'm sorry. Will you be okay?"

I fought back tears. "Oh, I'm fine. I'm glad you told me, but I really am tired, and I have a long day ahead of me tomorrow."

"Okay, I love you. Get some rest."

"I love you, too. Good night."

Sometimes, a person can get hit in the gut one too many times. For me, the news that Apollo had remarried was the sucker punch that floored me. I ended the call, pushed away from the nearly full plate of food, and collapsed into tears. I cried until I thought I'd run out of tears, and then I cried some more. The next morning, I was too exhausted to work. I called Kwame's assistant and told him I wasn't feeling well. I spent the day in bed and in tears.

12

"Bread of Heaven"

THREE DAYS PASSED. I SPENT THOSE THREE DAYS IN BED,
barely ate, and refused to answer my phone. I couldn't sleep…well,
at least not soundly. I was hurt when AJ broke the news about
Apollo's adultery. I was crushed when I heard him talking to Kay. I
was destroyed when he said those ugly things to me. But somehow,
knowing that he'd moved on and married Lisa had been the most
devastating blow. It made me feel like I had wasted all of those years
that we were together. It made me feel used and empty. I felt like all
of the love inside of me had been poured down a drain. I wasn't sure
if I had anymore to give.

Most of all, I was ashamed. Ashamed of how I was handling
things. I was known as the "Anointed Woman of God", and I
couldn't even get out a decent prayer. How many women had I
counseled? How many times had I prayed with the hurting and the

lost? Here I was, unable to take my own advice, too despondent to apply the Word that I knew so well to my own life.

To make matters worse, I didn't have the desire to sing at all. I used to love singing and ushering in His presence. Now I just wanted to lie in bed and disappear. It was sad and wrong, but it was true.

I pulled the covers over my head and whispered, "Lord, help me." In seconds I was in tears again. I cried and had nearly drifted off to sleep when a knock at the door startled me. I rose up in the bed and stared at the door. *Maybe they'll just go away.*

They didn't. The knocking continued for five or six more minutes. I released a frustrated sigh and without even checking myself in the mirror, trudged to the door and flung it open.

"*What?!*" I nearly screamed.

Standing before me, with raised eyebrows, was Kwame Kane. I looked down at my thin gown. "Give me a minute," I said. I shut the door and pulled on a pair of wrinkled jeans and a t-shirt and then let Kwame into the room.

He stopped just inside the door, but his scent traveled over to where I sat and filled my nose. He smelled like he'd just stepped out of the shower. He shoved his hands into the pockets of his jeans. "You've been under the weather?" He asked. He was an odd man. He spoke softly but at the same time, he seemed so confident. I'd never met anyone like him.

I nodded. "Look, Kwame, I've been going through some things

lately, and I honestly wasn't ready to get back in the studio when I was told to come here. I'm sorry I wasted your time."

He moved a little closer to me and ran his finger around the rim of his green turtle neck. The diamonds on his watch sparkled. "The people at the label have been calling, checking on our progress. I told them we had taken a little break, but that we'd get back to work today."

I shook my head. "I can't do it. I don't feel it anymore. I can't sing right now."

He walked over to me and crouched down beside me. "Can I tell you something, Ms. Langford?" *Gosh, he smells good.*

I looked at him for a moment and then nodded my head.

"You've always been on the short list of people I've wanted to work with. What you can do with your voice is amazing. I called and begged everyone I could think of to get a chance to work with you. So, if you would accompany me to the studio, you'd really be doing me a huge favor."

His voice was so soft and calm, almost soothing. I closed my eyes in an attempt to blink back tears. I failed. The next thing I knew, I was slumped over in my seat sobbing. Kwame reached up and wrapped his arms around me. I leaned against his shoulder. Though I'd only known him for a few days, it felt good to lean on him. It probably would've felt good to lean on anyone at that point.

I finally pulled myself together and sat up straight on the sofa. "You really meant what you said? You wanted to work with me that bad?"

He smiled. "I really meant it." He stood and took a seat beside me. "I know you're in pain. I heard about your father, the divorce. I'm sorry. But I think if you channel that pain into the music, we could really make some magic. You could turn this into a powerful testimony."

I offered him a weak smile. "You almost sound like a church boy."

"I *am* one. That's another reason I wanted to work with you. So, are you coming in to the studio today or am I gonna have to sound-proof this suite, cause I'll do it."

I laughed. "Give me about thirty minutes. I'll meet you there."

He stood from the sofa. "Thank you." He walked towards the door and then stopped and turned towards me. "The lab, in thirty minutes, right?"

I nodded. "I'll be there."

Before leaving that morning, I kneeled and prayed. For the first time since the divorce, I poured my heart out to God. I rose with a renewed desire to sing. And sing I did.

The next three days were very productive. No, that would be an understatement. Those three days were nothing short of *spectacular*. Something between Kwame and I just clicked. What we were creating was nearly beyond my comprehension, and I had never experienced a talent as great as his. There were times when I hated to leave the studio. I kind of wished that I could sit there all night and watch him work. I had greatly underestimated him. At this point, I wanted him to produce every track on the album, not just the five or six he'd agreed to.

I sat in the booth that Saturday evening with my eyes closed, listening to what we'd created earlier that day. Once the track faded out, the people crowding the studio, including the engineer and several musicians, began to applaud. I hung out there until only Kwame and I were left. He was waiting for feedback from the label. He's sent three songs to them earlier that day.

I looked up at him and smiled. He looked nervous, his eyes glued to his cell phone.

"You *can't* be nervous," I said.

He looked up at me and smiled. "I am. Just a little."

I shook my head. "I don't see why. You are a genius. You can't tell me you don't know that. I mean, you played most of the instruments on these songs, wrote and arranged all of the music. That's incredible."

He shrugged. "Well, I mean this is out of my comfort zone, really. I know what I'm capable of, but I've never done gospel before. I wanna do the right thing, you know? I don't wanna disrespect the genre *or* God."

I looked at him for a moment, surprised. Yes, Mr. Kane ran much deeper than I'd realized. "Well, I know gospel. What you've created is special and more than respectful. I believe that this music will touch many people who've never listened to Gospel music before. Think of how many souls could be saved. That's what it's all about."

"Yeah, you're right. I *am* good."

I rolled my eyes.

He laughed. "But seriously, if not for your gift, your *voice*, this music wouldn't be as special. I have the utmost respect for you, Ms. Langford."

"Call me Tonya. And thank you."

He looked me in the eye. "You're welcome."

We sat in silence for a few moments and then his phone rang. He checked the screen and gave me a thumbs-up as he answered it.

"Hello. Yes, George, good to hear from you. What did you think?" George Hoskins was the head of A&R at Calvary Records.

As Kwame listened, his eyes lit up. "Ok, ok, sure thing. I'll tell her. Thanks, George."

I waited anxiously as Kwame ended the call. He set his phone down and yelled, "Yes!!"

I laughed. "What is it? He liked it?"

"Liked it? He *loved* it! They want me to produce the entire album, if that's okay with you, of course," he said, excitedly.

"Yes! I mean that'd be fine with me."

Kwame jumped up and pulled me into a tight hug. "I didn't think I could do this! Thank you for letting me try," he said into my ear.

My skin tingled at feeling his warm breath against my skin. I closed my eyes and breathed in the scent of his cologne. Wait, what was I doing? Had I forgotten where I was? Once he released me, I stepped backward and smoothed the front of my blouse.

I cleared my throat. *Get yourself together. You just got rid of a man. You have no business thinking these types of thoughts about Kwame. You need to take your behind to church.*

I reclaimed my seat at the sound board and said, "Do you know of any good churches around here?"

He nodded as he reclaimed his own seat. "Yeah, you can come to mine."

"You go to church?" I was genuinely astonished.

"Wow, Ms.—I mean—Tonya, you think I'm some kind of demon or something?"

"Well, no…" I guess that *had* sounded kind of bad.

"It's okay. I don't guess it's common knowledge that I try to attend church as regularly as I can. If you want, I can pick you up in the morning, and we can go together."

I nodded. "That'd be great. I haven't been in a while." *Not since Apollo and I separated.*

"Great. Hey, we can have lunch together afterwards to celebrate. I know a place that makes the best whiting sandwiches."

"Ok, sounds good."

13

"Moving Forward"

I SAT NEAR THE REAR OF ST. PETER'S ROCK CHURCH,
Kwame's church in Newport News, Virginia. The church was
located just blocks from his studio. We made it there a few minutes
after service began. Kwame sat next to me with a smile on his face.
He seemed happy to be in church. I have to admit that I was pretty
happy myself. It had literally been months since I'd been in church,
and Lord knows I needed to hear a Word.

I smiled as I listened to Kwame sing along with the choir. I'd
noticed in the studio that Kwame had a decent singing voice. He
sounded nice as he blended in with the choir. I clapped and sang
along, careful to keep my voice low. People had been known to
request impromptu performances from me when they knew I was
present. I wasn't ready for that yet. I just wanted to worship God and
enjoy the service. And that I did.

I sat and listened attentively as the pastor brought a message from Matthew 11:29. *"Take my yoke upon you and learn from me, for I am gentle and humble in heart, and you will find rest for your souls"*. He spoke about resting in Jesus, casting our cares upon God, and finding peace in the midst of your storms. It was what my dad would call an "on-time word". I needed to hear it, and it nourished my soul.

After service, Kwame introduced me to the pastor. I don't think he recognized me, and I was grateful for that.

"Brother Kane!" he nearly shouted. "It's truly a blessing to see you here. I thought you'd be off somewhere working."

"Well, actually I'm working here in town right now, Pastor Adams. This is the artist I'm working with. Ms. Langford, this is my pastor, Reverend Lonnie Adams. Pastor Adams, this is Tonya Langford."

Pastor Adams smiled at me. "It's a blessing to meet you, sister." He turned back to Kwame and said, "How've you been, brother?"

"I'm doing pretty good. Taking it one day at a time."

Pastor Adams nodded. "I hear you, brother. Well I'll tell you this; your mother is missed here. She was such a wonderful woman."

Kwame smiled sweetly. "Thank you, Pastor. She loved this church and everything about it."

"God bless you, Brother Kane. You all have a blessed day."

"You too."

As we left the church, I smiled to myself. There was a lot about

Kwame Kane that I'd gotten wrong and even more that I had no idea about. One thing was for sure, I wanted to know it all. More and more, Mr. Kwame Kane was growing on me, and I liked it.

♪♪♪

I sat across from Kwame in the cramped booth and smiled as he placed our orders. We were at Young's Seafood Restaurant, a local favorite. Kwame rattled off an order of two Whiting sandwiches, fries, and sodas. When he was done, he looked at me and smiled.

"You know Tonya? This is the most I've seen you smile since you made it to Virginia."

"Well, I'm feeling pretty good, Mr. Kane."

"Kwame."

"Ok, Kwame. I enjoyed church. It was just what I needed."

"I'm glad. I've been a member of that church since my second year of college, which was also my last year of college. It was my mom's church after I moved her here."

I nodded. "Your mother passed away?"

Kwame eyes seemed to sadden in an instant. "About a year ago. She had a heart attack."

I reached across the table and rested my hand on top of his. "I'm sorry. Were you two close?"

"Yeah, she was my only family here. She was from Jamaica. She followed my dad here when she was pregnant with me. He died before I was born, so it was just me and her."

"No brothers or sisters?"

"Nope, just me."

"Wow, that must be hard for you. You know that I lost my dad last year, but my mom's still living, and I have three sisters."

"Yeah, I know."

I tilted my head and smiled. "You been researching me?"

If Kwame had been a few shades lighter-skinned, I might have thought he was blushing. "I guess you could say that."

"Well, what else do you know?"

"I know that you've been singing professionally since you were eight-years-old and that the Langford Sisters was one of the most successful Gospel groups in history. I also know that you've had a great solo career. And I've heard for myself that you have one of the most beautiful, anointed voices that God ever created."

I began to blush. "I see. Thank you. I did a little research on you, too."

He raised his eyebrows as if he was genuinely surprised. "Really? What did you find out?"

"Um, well, that the man I saw on those videos is not the Kwame Kane sitting across from me now."

He gave me a knowing smile. "Uh huh. What videos did you see?"

"Um, lets' see. 'Crank it Up' and 'Do It For Me'."

He laughed. "So you managed to watch the two videos where I was acting the biggest fool, huh?"

I laughed. "I guess so."

"Yeah well, a lot of that was just image, and some of it was the me that I was back then. I'm a different man now. Losing my mom changed me."

"Well, I have to apologize. I was actually dreading working with you."

"Yeah, I could tell from the way you were going off on the phone when I met you."

I dropped my eyes. I *had* acted a fool. "I was in a really bad place then. I'm better now. The work is helping. Your music is cathartic, really."

"Wow, well, thanks."

"I mean it. You're welcome."

The waitress delivered our meals, and we ended our conversation for the time being. I have to say that that was the best fish meal I'd had in a long time. I shared the sentiment with Kwame, who smiled and gave me an "I told you so." I enjoyed both the meal and the time with him. In the back of my mind, I kind of wished that our studio sessions wouldn't end. I really liked being around him. Kwame was calm and quiet and just plain kind. I needed that in my life.

Back in my room, I sat and thought about being in Virginia and working with Kwame. I thought about him sitting at his keyboard creating melodies in just a moment's time, then moving on to the drum set and creating the drum beats. He was a musical genius if there was really any such creature. I enjoyed watching him in action maybe even more than I enjoyed singing. He was truly amazing.

My cell phone buzzed. I checked the screen and smiled. It was Rebekah. "Hello. Hey, Beka."

"Hey, Ma. Wow, you sound chipper."

"I feel pretty good. I went to church with Kwame today."

"That's great. I know you were missing church."

"Yeah. How are things with you?"

"Um, Mama I hate to spoil your mood, but I've got something to tell you, and I don't want you to get mad at me."

I shook my head. Rebekah could be so dramatic about the smallest things sometimes. "What is it? Did you make a B on a test or something?" I joked.

I could hear Rebekah sigh through the phone. "Ma, this is serious."

"Okay, I'm sorry. Go ahead." I settled against the back of the sofa.

"I'm pregnant."

"W…what?"

"Mama, I'm pregnant." Rebekah began to sob. "I'm so sorry. I know you probably hate me for this."

I held the phone and closed my eyes. I was upset, and I can even admit that I was more than a little disappointed, but I knew that what

Beka needed right then was my support. "No, I don't hate you. I love you, and I always will. Nothing can change that. You'll get through this. *We'll* get through this."

"But I'll probably have to lay out of school for a while. I've messed everything up!"

"No, you haven't, sweetheart. It's alright."

"Ma, I...I didn't mean for this to happen. I really didn't. My life is ruined!"

"Beka, having a baby is not the end of the world. What about the father? How does he feel about this?"

"It's Keith. He says he's happy about it. He wants to get married." Keith had been her boyfriend since high school.

"What do *you* want?"

"I don't know."

"Well, you need to pray about this. Let the Lord lead you. I'll be praying, too."

"Okay. Thank you, Ma."

"Have you told your father yet?"

"Yeah. He was really upset."

As if he has the right to be upset, I thought. "Well, he'll be okay. Just pray. Everything will work out."

"Okay. I love you, Mama."

"I love you, too."

That evening there were several things on my mind. I was concerned about Rebekah's situation—another blow. I prayed for her and afterwards, I felt like things would be okay with her. And no matter how I tried, I couldn't get Kwame off of my mind. What was going on with me?

14

"Trading My Sorrows"

I PEERED OUT OF THE CAR WINDOW AS I RODE TOWARDS the Embassy Suites in Hampton. I had been in Virginia for three and a half weeks. Three and half weeks of musical bliss. A short time, but time enough for me to have developed feelings for Kwame Kane. I rubbed my forehead as that same foreboding thought returned. *Was I just trying to replace Apollo?* I was lonely. I may as well admit that. After all, I was married for twenty years. I was used to having the companionship of another. I was accustomed to the comforting arms of a man after a long trip or a rough day in the studio.

I missed kisses and hugs, no matter how fake they may have been. But, who was I fooling? Kwame was a very eligible bachelor. I was sure that women were chasing him down left and right, vying for a chance to become Mrs. Kwame Kane, with others willing to be known only as his "baby mama". I hadn't seen any women other than his employees around the studio, but what did that mean?

I learned a lot about Kwame over those three weeks. He was kind and considerate. He was a musical genius, and he was a fan of mine. But I didn't have a clue if he had a girlfriend or wife or kids. Part of me needed to know and another part of me was afraid to know...afraid of being disappointed.

I smiled at the driver as he opened the door for me. I'd been doing a lot of smiling, and I knew I could thank God for that, and Kwame had a little to do with it, too. I made my way to my room slowly. I had really hated to leave the studio, but it was creeping towards midnight, and Kwame had insisted that I come back to the hotel and get some sleep. We were gonna start working early in the morning. We had to wrap things up in a week or so because he had another project pending.

Inside my suite, I showered and dressed for bed. I wasn't hungry so I decided to read my Bible and pray. Afterwards, I sat in the bed and grabbed my notebook from the bedside table. Twenty minutes later, I'd finished writing a song. I read over it and thought, *thank you, Jesus.* I fell into a sweet, sweet sleep with no trouble.

The next morning, I was up at the crack of dawn. I was anxious to share the song with Kwame. I knew exactly which track it would go perfectly with. I dressed, had breakfast, and beat Kwame to the studio. I was sitting in the waiting area when he arrived. He was wearing black slacks and a white oxford shirt with white sneakers. His dread locs were pulled back into a ponytail. He smiled that shiny metal smile and nearly made me melt. I'd always reveled at Apollo's good looks and physique. Apollo could stop traffic at noon in the middle of New York City. Kwame was different. He wasn't "drop dead" gorgeous, but he was growing more and more attractive to me day by day. He had a way about him that made him much more striking, more magnetic than Apollo had ever been to me. I was drawn to Kwame.

"Reporting to work early, eh?" he said, removing his dark eyeglasses.

I nodded. "Good morning." I was smiling so widely that my cheeks hurt. Gosh, I was really too old to be feeling like this.

"Good morning to you. Ready to work?"

I stood and followed him into the studio with my notebook in hand, breathing in his expensive cologne every step of the way. "I sure am. I wrote a little something last night. I think it'll go good with that track you played for me the other week. You know, the one with the stringed instruments."

He nodded. "Alright then, let's hear it."

A few moments later I stood in the recording booth. I took a deep breath as the beautifully orchestrated music played. Once the intro was over, I began to sing,

"I can't take another step or breathe another breath

My burdens, Dear Lord, are too heavy
And though I know You're there
Because You're everywhere
Oh Father, it feels like You've left me

My greatest desire is to sense Your presence
My most urgent need is to feel Your touch

And Lord, I'm sorry that my faith is so weak
But right now I need You so much

You see, Lord, it's only You who can see me through
Only Your loving touch can heal me

Only You can bring me through
You alone know how to love me
Only You... only You...only You..."

It was another of those rare instances when Kwame let me sing through in one take. No breaks, no suggestions, no tweaks. I had memorized the words because they were from my heart, so I sang with my eyes closed. When I was finished, I opened them and watched as Kwame shook his head and then turned and left the studio. I sat on the stool inside the booth and wiped my tears, sure that Kwame was outside the room doing the same thing. I'd felt it, and I knew that anyone who'd been listening had felt the same thing.

It was as if God had walked into that studio and smiled on all of us. I was full. Full of love for God. Full of hope and full of joy. It wasn't long before I'd dropped to my knees right there in that booth and began to pray a prayer of thanksgiving. In that studio, in those moments, I'd experienced my breakthrough. I don't know how long I prayed, but when I arose from the floor, Kwame was back in the room at his customary position behind the mixing board. The engineer was gone. I climbed onto the stool and watched as Kwame stood and walked into the booth. He closed the door behind him and leaned against it.

"Uh, you okay?" he asked softly.

I nodded. "Better than I've been in a long time. You?"

He shoved his hands in the pockets of his pants. His eyes were wide as he said, "Yeah, I guess. I've never felt anything like that before."

I smiled. "That was God's presence. His power."

"I heard my mama talk about it but, up until now, never felt it. It was powerful *and* overwhelming."

"It's overwhelming because it commands attention. There's no way you can ignore His presence."

"Definitely not. I feel gutted."

I smiled again. "Not gutted. He just emptied some stuff out of you to make room for more of Him."

He nodded. "Oh, okay."

"Well, what do you want to work on next?"

"I was thinking that we could call it a day. I, for one, need time to recuperate."

"Oh, okay. Well, let me call the driver." I pulled my cell phone out of my pocket.

"I'll take you."

It was only a short drive from Kwame's studio to the hotel.

Kwame's SUV was filled with silence as he drove. It wasn't an awkward silence, but more of a peaceful one. I think both of us were so full and satisfied that there was just nothing for us to say. Once we made it to the hotel, Kwame walked me to my door. We said our goodbyes and made plans to resume our work in the morning.

I sat on the edge of the bed and sighed. I honestly did not feel like spending an entire day in that room. I needed to sight-see or shop or something, anything other than sit alone in that room. I sat there for a few moments and then decided to head downstairs. I was going to see if I could get some information about the area, maybe find something to do or somewhere to go. I grabbed my key card, opened the door, and nearly jumped out of my skin. Kwame was standing at the door.

"Good Lord, Kwame! You scared me half to death!"

He shrugged and gave me a lopsided grin. "I'm sorry."

"What are you doing?"

"I...I didn't want to be alone."

I looked at him for a moment then said, "Me either." We just stood there. I guess neither one of us knew what to do or say next.

Finally, Kwame said, "You wanna go get something to eat?"

I nodded. "Okay, that sounds good. Fish again?"

He gave me a shiny smile. "I had a little something different in mind."

♫♫♫

I guess my idea of different was a little different from Kwame's. I was thinking maybe steak or chicken. You know? Something different from seafood. Kwame was thinking different as in a different city. Well, actually, a different country. It seemed that Mr. Kane had a taste for Jamaican cuisine. And to him, the best place to get it was in Jamaica. I wasn't turning down a trip to Jamaica. That was for sure. As I sat on his private jet, I had to marvel at his sense of spontaneity. I'd said I wanted to get out of that room, and I was definitely out of that room!

I sat across from him and watched as he played with his phone or texted or whatever he was doing. The more I looked at him, the more he appealed to me. He adjusted his body in his seat and scratched the stubble on his chin. His expensive watch slid down towards his wrist as he lowered his hand and continued to tinker with his phone. I studied his every move. I was intrigued by everything he did. He smiled at whatever he was reading. I smiled because he smiled.

I clasped my hand to my mouth. What was I doing? Did I have a crush on Kwame? I hadn't felt this giddy or silly since before I married Apollo. This was not any way for a respectable woman to be acting or feeling, was it? *This man has got to have a girlfriend. Ask him.*

I cleared my throat. Kwame's head popped up. "You checking in with your girlfriend?" I'd said it. *Now I feel silly.*

He shook his head. "Reading a text from my daughter."

"Daughter? I didn't know you had kids."

"You need to do your research. I have 10 kids, actually." My heart dropped. *10? What kind of man has 10 kids?*

"Uh, really? 10?"

He laughed. "Nah, just one. Aresha. She's 12."

"Oh." *Phew.*

He clicked a button on the phone and then reached over and handed it to me. "This is her."

I looked at the picture on the screen. The girl was a shade lighter than Kwame's dark brown skin, but she greatly resembled him.

"She's beautiful. She looks a lot like you."

He smiled. "Yeah, unfortunately she *does* look like me. I was hoping she'd take after her mom since she's a model."

I raised my eyebrows as I handed him his phone. "A model? Really? You two been together long?"

He laid the phone on his thigh. "Oh, we're not together anymore."

"Oh, well I know how hard divorce is. Is Aresha coping pretty well?"

He shifted in his seat. "Now I'm embarrassed. Her mother, Yvette, and I were never married. We dated for a couple of years and split shortly after Aresha was born."

"Oh, I see. It happens that way sometimes."

"But not with you, huh? You're a preacher's kid. You did everything in the right order, didn't you?"

I settled against the back of the seat. "I thought I did. It turns out that not much was in right order, after all. Oh well, you live and learn."

Kwame nodded. "You got that right."

15

"Made Me Glad"

JAMAICA IS PARADISE ON EARTH. IT LOOKS, FEELS, AND
smells like paradise. It is simply a beautiful place full of beautiful
people. I smiled and soaked in the rays of the sun as we exited the
plane and walked across the tarmac to the waiting car. It was warm
and inviting. In an instant, I felt right at home.

Kwame's face lit up once the plane hit the ground. It was as if
Jamaica was his lifeline. He chattered on and on during the drive
through Kingston to his home. He pointed out various sites, serving
as an adequate tour guide.

Kwame smiled as the car pulled onto a rocky path. "We're almost
there," he said softly.

"Your house?" I asked.

"My *paradise*."

I peered out the window as we traveled down the rocky path, past palm and breadfruit trees. My eyes widened when Kwame's house came into view. It was a stilted white cottage, sitting right on the beach. A porch wrapped around the entire house. The sun bathed the cottage as if serving as its natural spotlight. Behind the house I could see the blue ocean as it crashed against the beach. It looked like a perfect postcard.

As we stepped out of the car, my nose was greeted by the scent of the pink and white hibiscuses lining the narrow pathway that led to the steps. I closed my eyes and smiled. "Look at what my God has done. It is so beautiful here," I said.

Kwame smiled at me and took my hand, leading me up the steps. "The first time I came here, I thought the same thing. I love it here."

"I can see why."

As we stepped onto the porch, I noted the Adirondack chairs and potted plants that crowded the porch, adding a homey appeal to the house. The wooden front door was open, but the screen door was shut. I could smell that someone was cooking up a storm inside

Kwame opened the screen door. "Well, come on in. Smells like Fefe's just about done with dinner."

"Fefe?"

"My aunt, Feona. She takes care of the place when I'm not here. I asked her to fix us dinner."

Fefe was a short woman with wide hips and a bright smile. Her smooth dark brown skin and expressive eyes matched Kwame's. She was the sister of Kwame's mother. She was friendly and very talkative. I had trouble understanding much of what she said to me, and I'm sure that she had the same problem understanding my southern accent, but Kwame provided great translations for both of us.

One thing I understand in any language is food. I hadn't ever flown thousands of miles for a meal before, but this one was definitely worth it. Jerk chicken, rice and peas, coco bread—all Kwame's favorites. Ooo wee! Ms. Fefe could burn! I ate until I came very close to gluttony, and then I settled down on a beach chair next to Kwame and watched the waves crash against the beach.

"Thank you for this. I just wish I'd packed something. You'll probably get sick of seeing me in these same old rags."

"We'll leave in the morning. I'm sure Aunt Fefe's got something you can wear on the trip back. Y'all are about the same size, huh?"

I shrugged. "I guess so." I actually thought that Aunt Fefe was smaller than me, but we'd see.

We sat in silence for a moment and then I said, "So, this is home, huh?"

"Yah mon! 'Tis be ware me people are." We both laughed.

"How in the world did you get from Jamaica to Newport News, Virginia?"

"College. I was raised in New York—Queens. I was actually a pretty good student in high school, and I got a scholarship to Hampton U. I liked Virginia, so when I decided to buy a home, I bought one in Virginia. Bought one for my mom there, too."

"That's sweet."

"Yeah, she thought so, too."

"Do you have any pictures of her?"

Kwame nodded, stood from his seat, and headed into the house. Minutes later, he emerged with a framed photo in hand. He handed it to me and then settled back into his seat. It was a photo of Kwame and his mother. It looked like they were standing in front of the cottage. She wore a flowing white dress and a white flower in her long salt-and-pepper hair. She was smiling brightly with her arm around Kwame. She was a strikingly beautiful woman. She and Kwame were the same height and shared the same dark brown skin and the same eyes, but that's where the similarities ended. Kwame's other features must've have been inherited from his father.

I handed the photo back to him. "She was beautiful, Kwame."

He held the photo in his hand and stared at it for a moment and then nodded. "She was. She passed away a few months after this was taken. She loved this house."

"I do, too."

He smiled at me, but I could still see sadness in his eyes. "I'm glad you do."

We sat in silence, and then I said, "Are there a lot of Kanes still around here?"

"Ah, now I must reveal an ancient secret. I'm not a Kane."

I frowned. "You're not?"

"Nope, my real name is Clinton Francis. Kwame Kane's my stage name."

I raised my eyebrows. "Seriously?"

"Yah. Me be de baby boy of Marietta and Waymon Francis," he said, putting on a thick Jamaican accent.

"Why'd you change it?"

"Well, when I first started out trying to break into the music business, I didn't think anyone would take 'Clinton Francis' seriously. So I made up this crazy name, 'Kwame Ko Kane'. Eventually I dropped the 'Ko'. I've been Kwame Kane ever since."

"Mmhmm. I see."

"My mom never called me Kwame, though. She hated that I used a different name. She always called me Clinton. When she said it, it was like she pronounced ever single letter. Like every letter was important. 'Clin-ton!' she'd say. 'C'mere buoy!'" he laughed.

I smiled. "You really miss her, don't you?"

"I do. She was the best."

"I bet she was proud of you."

He shrugged. "For the most part. She'd have been prouder if she could've heard what we're working on together and if she could've seen the changes I've made on my life now. That's what she wanted. She was worried about me." He shook his head.

"Well, the Kwame I see is a good man. I can't understand why she'd be worried."

He gave me half of a smile. "Thanks, but I used to be pretty wild.

Partying all night, drinking, drugs. You name it, I did it. You wouldn't have thought I was good if you knew me then."

"Oh, I see."

"You don't know anything about that stuff, huh?"

I shrugged. "Not first hand."

He nodded. "Yeah, you just seem to have lived this perfect life. No drinking, no drugs, no problems."

I laughed bitterly. "I thought my life was perfect, too. Then I lost my daddy. My kid got arrested. My marriage fell apart. Now, I find out that my daughter's pregnant, and I really thought that she had it together. It makes me wonder if anything is really as it seems."

"Not usually."

I looked him in the eye. "Then how do you live? If everything around you is an illusion, how do you live? Who do you trust? That's what I'm struggling with now. I mean, I'm better than I was, but it still hurts. I thought I was doing the right thing, singing and travelling, but now I think maybe I should've stayed home more, spent more time with my kids. And to think that my husband, the only man I knew and loved for more than twenty years, was sleeping with tons of women, and he even got one pregnant! He's a man of God! What do I do with that? How can I recognize reality when everyone around me is wearing masks and playing roles?"

Kwame cleared his throat, "Um I—"

I shook my head. "Why am I even telling you all of this? Thank you for everything. I'm going to bed. I'll be ready to leave in the morning." I didn't wait for him to answer. I walked back into the house, thanked Aunt Fefe for the meal, and headed to the guest bedroom. I managed not to cry. I just kneeled beside the bed, closed my eyes, and prayed. As I stood to climb into the bed, I heard a soft knock at the door.

"Yes? Who is it?"

"Kwame."

I opened the door. He stepped into the room and closed the door behind him. "I think you did the best you knew how with your family, and I'm sorry that your husband hurt you. I was wrong, you know," he said softly.

"About what?"

"About things usually being other than as they seem. I think you're a wonderful woman. You are so talented, and I can see that you have a good heart. *He* was the illusion, not you. You're real."

"Thank you, Kwame."

He kissed me on the cheek. "Goodnight, Tonya."

"Goodnight."

He headed to the door and then stopped. I watched as he turned around and walked back towards me. He kissed me softly on the lips. I kissed him back. Then I cried.

♪♪♪

I woke up and smiled. The scent of Kwame's cologne still lingered in the room. I thought about the kiss and the way he'd held me when I cried. The words he'd whispered into my ear to comfort me. I rolled over and felt his warm body. I stretched my arm across his chest—wait, his chest? I bolted upright in the bed. I looked over at Kwame lying next to me, fast asleep. I jumped out of the bed and stumbled towards the light switch on the wall. What in the name of everything holy had happened up in here?!

Kwame's eyes popped open. "You okay?" he asked.

"Oh dear Lord in heaven, what did we do? What did *I* do?" I was distraught. Up to that point I could honestly say that I'd never had premarital sex. I'd never fornicated. *Never.*

Kwame sat up in the bed. We both still had our clothes on. Had we redressed? How could I have had sex and then redressed with no recollection of any of it happening?

"What's wrong?" he asked groggily.

"Did I—I mean—did we…"

He shook his head. "No, no. We fell asleep, that's it. I didn't wanna leave you alone. You want me to go now?"

"Yes—I mean—no." I closed my eyes and shook my head. "Lord, I don't know."

He stood and walked over to me. He placed his hands on my arms. "I'll go. You get some rest." He kissed my forehead.

I went back to bed. I closed my eyes, but found no sleep. I wished he'd stayed. I wished I knew what I wanted.

16

"It Ain't Over"

THE PLANE RIDE BACK TO VIRGINIA WAS QUIET. I GUESS
neither one of us knew what to say or how to feel. I liked Kwame.
That much I couldn't deny. But I was confused and conflicted. I
mean, did I really need to be thinking about another man when I was
still getting over Apollo? I think that part of me still loved Apollo,
even if just a little bit.

Once I made it back to my room, I took a nap. I was supposed to
meet Kwame in the studio a little later on. I woke up feeling
refreshed and ready to work.

I hopped out of bed, then showered and dressed. I was eating a
light brunch when I heard my phone ring.

"Hello?"

"Hey Ma." It was AJ.

"AJ! Boy, I thought you'd disappeared off the face of the earth.

You too grown to call your Mama now?"

"Aw Mama. I'm calling you now, ain't I?"

"AJ, I've been up here for nearly a month, and this is my first time hearing from you."

"Yeah, sorry about that. I been kinda busy."

"Busy doing what? How's school?"

"A'ight."

"How're your grades, AJ?"

"Okay."

I sighed. He was hiding something. But I knew AJ. He wasn't going to reveal whatever it was until he was ready. It didn't matter how much I pushed him.

"Okay, well, things are going really well here."

"Yeah, The Swami's a beast. He gone have you all up in the R&B charts."

I smiled. "Kwame's definitely good. But I don't know about all that R&B stuff."

"Hey, get me an autograph or something. Tell him I'm a fan."

"Sure will. Who knows, maybe you'll get to meet him one day."

"That'd be cool. Um, Ma?"

"Yes?"

"I love you."

I smiled again. "I love you, too."

We hung up, and I called and checked on Mama and Tennille and got a good report on everyone. I called Beka. She was still doing good. I grabbed my purse and headed out the door. I smiled as I climbed into the car. I smiled all the way to Swami Productions.

♪♪♪

I sat next to Kwame, listening to the rough edits of the fourteen songs we'd created together. They were phenomenal even in their unfinished state. I bobbed my head to the beat of an up-tempo song and glanced over at Kwame. He was sitting still with his hand on his chin, staring at nothing in particular. In the short time we'd worked together, I recognized that look. The wheels were turning in his brain. He was thinking of something. Knowing him, it was something brilliant and ingenious.

The track ended and Kwame looked up at me. "I've got an idea for this one."

I nodded. "Okay." I trusted him. He definitely knew what he was doing.

"This track kind of reminds me of one of your older songs. One you did with your sisters."

I knew what he was referring to. "Yeah, it does sound kinda like 'Shout for Joy'."

"That's the one! I was thinking that maybe your sisters could sing with you on this one. The harmony would be crazy! It'd be like a reunion song."

I froze. What was I supposed to say to that? What could I have said that wouldn't reveal my family business? "Um, that's a good idea, but my sisters are busy with their own lives. I doubt if they'd want to leave their homes and fly here."

He was too excited to be deterred. "Well, where do they live? Maybe we could set something up at another studio. I've got connections all over the country."

I shifted my weight on the stool and rubbed my hands on my thighs. "Uh…Atlanta. They all live in or near Atlanta."

"Great! I've got a good friend who has a studio there. Let me call him."

Before I could reply, Kwame had hopped out of his seat and bolted out of the door. I sat there and waited. *Lord, I can't ask them to do this.* Toi and Theresa still wouldn't so much as speak to me.

Kwame came back into the studio. "My friend, Tiger, says we're free to use his studio anytime we want. Did you call your sisters?"

"Um…Kwame…I don't think this'll work. My sisters and I don't exactly have the best relationship."

He gave me a confused look. "Why?"

I clasped my hands in my lap and sighed. "Um, I kinda left the group hanging after I married my ex-husband. They tried to keep going without me, but they weren't very successful."

"And you were, huh?"

I nodded. "Only one of them will even talk to me now, and we just reconnected after our father passed."

He leaned forward and took my hand in his. "Then maybe it's time for you to reach out to them. If it was leaving the group that tore you guys apart, maybe a reunion can bring you back together."

Maybe he was right, but I doubted it.

♫♫♫

I was a nervous wreck during the flight to Atlanta. I'd already told Tennille what Kwame had in mind. She'd quickly agreed and volunteered to run the idea by Toi and Theresa. I hadn't checked back with her. I was too anxious about the whole thing. I'd just wait until I got there. If push came to shove, I'd record the song as a duet with Tennille. Our voices were always the most compatible anyway.

We landed and made our way to my mom's house in Kwame's rented car. I was a basket case. What if my sisters thought I was trying to use them to sell records? What if they went off on me? What would my mother say? What would Kwame think? I sighed as I walked up to the front door and rang the doorbell. Kwame rested his hand on my shoulder. I gave him a weak smile.

"Tony!" Tennille yelled as she opened the door and pulled me into a tight hug.

I smiled and hugged her back. So many times in the past I'd wished for a hug like that. It was good to finally get one.

"Hey, Tennille! This is Mr. Kwame Kane. Kwami, this is my baby sister, Tennille Langford."

Kwami smiled widely and shook Tennille's hand. "Great to meet you, Tennille."

Tennille smiled and nodded. "Well, y'all come on in." She grabbed my arm and steered me towards the living room. "So he's a big-time producer, huh?" she whispered. "Is he single?"

I nodded. "Yeah, I think so." *And I'm crazy about him.*

"Good," she continued to whisper. "I'm tired of being a Langford." She twisted her head around and shot Kwame a smile. I shook my head.

17

"Glorious"

I SAT ON THE SOFA IN MY PARENTS' LIVING ROOM NEXT TO Tennille, and I was a ball of nerves. Across from us sat Theresa and Toi. While Tennille and I shared most of the same features, Toi and Theresa had inherited our father's fair brown complexion and piercing brown eyes. Theresa was the oldest and she was gorgeous. She wore her sandy hair in a precise bob that fell just below her chin. As usual, her make-up was flawless. Her husband, Greg, was an executive with Coca-Cola. He took very good care of Theresa and her Chanel dress and Prada shoes were evidence of that.

Toi was the second oldest. After her came me, then Tennille. Toi was more Bohemian. She was my only other sister who wore her natural hair. With her soft afro picked out to its full potential, she could pass for a slightly older version of Esperanza Spaulding. She wore faded jeans and a t-shirt. She could have easily passed for a woman half her age. Her husband, Stanley, was an artist. They'd never had any children.

We sat there face to face for the first time since our father's funeral. Our mother sat to the side of us, in our father's easy chair. I spoke first.

"Um, thank you guys for agreeing to hear me out."

That statement was met with a heavy silence. Tension hung in the air like the humidity on a balmy summer's day.

I cleared my throat, crossed my legs, and continued. "Um, well, first, I want to apologize if I've ever done anything to hurt any of you. You're my sisters, and I love you. I…I really want for us to reconnect and be a real family again."

"*And* you want us to sing on some song?" Toi said as she rolled her eyes. Her voice bore the evidence of her displeasure with me.

I twisted my bracelet on my wrist. It was one that Apollo had bought for me a few years earlier. I wasn't sure why I still wore it. "Um, well, it would be great if you all would sing with me, but that's not the most important thing. I want us to get along again. I've missed you guys."

It was Theresa's turn to speak. "That's funny. You didn't seem to miss us as long as you had your precious Apollo. You get a divorce, and all of a sudden you want to reconnect with us. I don't buy it." She turned to Toi, then Tennille. "I think she's trying to use us. I'm not falling for it."

I glanced at my mother who was looking down at the floor. I looked back across at my sisters and shook my head. "I'm not trying to use anyone. I have no reason to. My career is not in trouble. I'll be honest, though. My divorce put a lot of things into perspective for me. I realize that I should've done this a long time ago, *years* ago. I guess I was too scared or too stubborn. I don't know. But I'm trying to do it now. If you refuse to forgive me, I'll just have to accept it and move on."

Theresa and Toi looked at each other. Then both of them looked at me. No one said anything for a while until my mother spoke up. "Girls, I love you all. But one thing your father's death has taught me is that life is too short to hold grudges. Tony is doing the right thing, trying to make amends. If you two refuse to forgive her, that sin will lay at your door—not hers. You know the Word. We are commanded to forgive. It's not optional." She stood from her seat. "I'm leaving. You all settle this today. Tomorrow's not promised." We all watched as she left the room. We sat in silence for a while longer.

Tennille hopped up from the sofa. "Look y'all. I was probably the angriest of all of us at her. I was only fifteen when we broke up. I loved singing and travelling, and I only got to do it for a little while. I think she was doing what she thought was right at the time. Right or wrong, what happened is in the past."

Theresa shook her head. "She deserted us. She went on performing and recording like we didn't even exist. She never once invited us along on a tour or to do a show. It hurt to be left out like that. That group was my life!"

Tennille moved closer to Theresa with her hands on her wide hips. "Terry, you know good and well that you were sick of the road. You were always whining about how you missed Greg and the twins. You were ready to quit the group anyway." Terry was Theresa's nickname.

Theresa dropped her eyes to the floor. "That doesn't change the fact that what she did was wrong. She just quit the group with no warning."

Tennille wasn't backing down. "Would it really have mattered if she'd told us months in advance? The outcome would've been the same. Come on, we're supposed to be Christians, preacher's kids. You can't forgive your sister? How about you Tiny?" Tiny was Toi's nickname. She'd never weighed any more than 115 pounds in her life.

"Look, 'Nill. I forgive her." She looked me in the eye. "*I forgive you*, Tony. I did a long time ago. It just still hurts. You went on to have this huge career. I can't help but wonder how things might have turned out if the group had stayed together."

I sighed. "You can't be saying that you're jealous of me! Yes, I've had a successful career. I've spent my life travelling the world. I'm proud of the work I do for God, but now I realize that I had things out of order. I didn't have to be famous to do His work *or* His will. I could've been just as effective witnessing in my husband's church and ministering in my own home. You guys still have your families intact. I lost my sisters, who were my best friends. I lost touch with my father, who was my heart. My marriage was a sham from the start, and now I've lost that, too. My children are mixed up. Yeah, I'm famous and successful, but at what cost?"

I paused and shook my head. "I'd really like for you all to forgive me. I'd really like for us to sing together. I'm truly sorry. If I could go back and change things, I would. But I can't. *I can't...*" I collapsed against the back of the sofa and covered my face with my hands. I didn't want to cry in front of them, but it was too late. The tears were flowing freely. I couldn't stop them. I didn't *want* to stop them.

I felt arms around me. Tennille. Thank God she'd forgiven me. Another pair of arms embraced me and then another. I moved my hands and looked around me. All three of my sisters were holding on to me, comforting me. I closed my eyes and held my head back. *Thank You, Lord!* I continued to cry tears of joy and thanksgiving. *Thank You, Lord for bringing my family back together.*

18

"Grateful"

TENNILLE AND I ARRIVED AT TIGER TOWNSEND'S STUDIO in Decatur a little earlier than Toi and Theresa. I walked into the studio that Kwame had reserved for us and instantly began to smile. He was sitting at the mixing board with Fred. Kwame looked like a breath of fresh air, wearing khaki cargo pants and a white polo shirt. When he heard us walk in, he looked up and smiled. His braces gleamed. His dread locks swung with his head.

"Hey! You made it." He walked over and pulled me into a tight hug. I closed my eyes and hugged him back. He felt good, *too good.* I didn't want that hug to end.

We finally parted, and I said, "Well, Tennille and I are ready to work."

He smiled at Tennille. "Great! I'm so glad you guys are here. Tennille, this is my engineer, Fred. Fred, this is half of the famous

Langford sisters." Fred and Tennille shook hands and I think I saw Fred checking her out.

With what amounted to a permanent smile on my face, I said, "Theresa and Toi should be here any minute."

He moved closer to me and whispered, "See, I told you it would work out."

I looked at him and nodded. "You did. Thank you."

He smiled again. "No problem. Um, Tennille, let me get you the lyrics. The song is called 'To You'. Me and your sister wrote it."

Tennille flashed him her best smile. "Oh, okay. Then it must be great."

Kwame and Fred left us alone in the studio, and Tennille swatted me on the arm.

"Ow! What was that for?!" I asked as I rubbed my arm.

"Why didn't you tell me you two had something going on? Here I was ready to bag him. You shoulda told me, Tony!"

"What are you talking about, 'Nill? He's not even my type."

"What? He's not as pretty as Apollo? Apollo was like a shiny red apple with a rotten core. Anyway, you sure are *his* type. He lit up like a Christmas tree when he saw you."

I sighed and lowered my voice. "Okay, honestly I do kinda like him, but I'm still trying to piece my life back together right now. I don't think I need to be starting any new relationships."

"Well, it looks to me like it's already started. If you like him, and he *obviously* likes you, then I don't see any harm in it. You're a grown woman, and Kwame seems like a nice guy. Plus, Apollo's not letting any grass grow under his feet."

I shook my head. "No, he's definitely not."

Thankfully, Toi and Theresa arrived in time to interrupt that little conversation. We all hugged and chatted a little before Kwame returned and put us to work.

♪♪♪

I stood at the microphone and smiled as I looked around at my sisters. It felt like old times, like we were young again and excited about singing for the Lord. My heart was full. It wasn't hard for me to sing the lyrics.

Heavenly Father
So real you are to me
Dear precious savior
How much to me you mean

Your love is so real
Oh, how You make me feel
Like there's nothing I can't do
So today, I'm gonna lift my voice to you… …

I finished the first two verses and my sisters joined in on the chorus:

I lift my voice to You
It's the very least I can do
My reasonable sacrifice, knowing that You gave Your life
I lift my voice to You!

I looked up and saw that Kwame was grinning from ear to ear and bobbing his head to the energizing beat. I squeezed my eyes shut and smiled as Tennille sang the second and third verses. Toi and Theresa took turns with the bridge, and we all sang the chorus together again. I was in heaven. Our harmony was just as beautiful as if we'd never stopped singing together. I thanked God again. I was so grateful.

19

"Celebrate"

I SAT IN FIRST CLASS NEXT TO KWAME AND CLOSED MY eyes. The trip had gone so well. It was the best time I could remember having in Atlanta in a long while. I'd reconnected with my sisters, and I couldn't have been happier. I felt like some of the holes in my heart had finally been plugged up. I was so thankful for that.

"Why does your family call you Tony?" Kwame's voice broke into my thoughts.

I smiled at him. "Well, my daddy wanted a boy so bad. When I came along, they already had two girls. My dad wanted to name me Tony, after his brother if I was a boy. He convinced himself that I would be a boy and called me Tony the whole time my mom was pregnant with me. When I ended up being a girl, he kept on calling me Tony. My mama added the 'a' at the end, and it became Tonya, but I've always been Tony to my family."

"Then came Tennille, huh? Still no boy," Kwame said.

"Yep. Four girls, no boys."

"You guys are all so talented. Being in the studio with you all was like watching a master class on harmonizing. He must've been proud of his girls."

I nodded. "He was."

"Can I call you Tony?"

I looked him directly in his eyes. I'd never noticed before how beautiful they were. His eyes were small and almond-shaped with the thickest eyelashes. I could get lost in his eyes. "If you want to," I said.

He smiled at me.

"Kwame, can I ask *you* something?"

He nodded. "Sure."

"What's with the braces?"

He laughed loudly, as if I'd told a hilarious joke. "Why? Do they bother you?"

"Well, no. I've just never seen a grown man with braces, and they're not even the invisible kind."

"Um, well back in the day I used to wear grills."

"Grills?"

"Yeah, I had a platinum grill, a diamond-encrusted grill. Hell, I wore a different grill nearly every day of the week. Anyway, they messed up the alignment of my teeth. So, now I have to wear braces, and my orthodontist said I couldn't wear the invisible kind. That's why I'm a brace-face."

I nodded. "Oh, okay."

We sat there silently for a while, and then Kwame grasped my hand. I looked over at him and smiled. We held hands all the way back to Virginia.

♪♪♪

The day I'd dreaded finally came. It was our last day in the studio. In all, we'd created thirty songs together. It would be up to the record execs and me to decide how many of them would actually end up on the CD. I was both excited and sad. I was looking forward to releasing the album, but I hated to leave Virginia and Kwame.

We sat together and listened to song after song. We'd created something different and beautiful. I was amazed at how good everything sounded. When the final track had faded out, Kwame smiled as me and reached for my hand.

"We did it, Tony. It's a masterpiece, if I do say so myself."

I nodded in agreement. "It's beautiful, *wonderful*. Thank you for working with me."

He shook his head. "*Thank you.* I'm grateful for the chance to work with you." He looked into my eyes for so long that I finally dropped my gaze. It felt like he was looking right through me.

"Let's celebrate with dinner tonight," he said.

"Well, my flight's kinda early tomorrow morning. I don't know,"

I said, suddenly feeling nervous.

"We can have dinner at my house, and I promise I won't keep you out late."

I hesitated, and then said, "Okay."

"Great! I'll have someone pick you up."

Kwame's house was a Tudor-style waterfront estate that looked like it belonged in the English countryside instead of in Newport News. Hidden behind a wrought iron fence and tall hedges, with the Chesapeake Bay as a backdrop, the house was breathtaking. As I rode along in the back of the SUV, peering through the tinted windows, I wondered just how much money a person could make producing records. One thing was for sure, Kwame had done well for himself, *very* well.

Inside the house was just as gorgeous as outside. It was different from the cottage in Jamaica. In Jamaica, his home had a more airy, loose feel to it. It felt like a place where you could relax and enjoy yourself with no end in sight. His home in Virginia was statelier. With shiny dark hardwood floors, expensive-looking heavy drapes, and dark leather furniture that filled the living room, the house looked like it belonged to a king or someone who'd grown up with a lot of money and prestige.

I was sitting on the overstuffed sofa in his living room, staring at the platinum plaques lining the wall. How many of those did he have? I turned my head and eyed the shelf that held numerous awards. There were three Grammys. Three! I only had two, and *I* was a singer. Kwame was successful, alright. I was amazed at the magnitude of his success.

"You ready to eat?" Kwame said. He was standing in the doorway to the living room. He wore a pair of black slacks and a red dress shirt. His hair hung freely just below his shoulders. He was smiling. I returned his smile.

"I didn't know this was a formal affair," I said. I was wearing a pair of jeans and a pink blouse.

He shrugged. "It's not. I just wanted to look nice for you."

I blushed. "Oh, okay. Thank you."

He walked over to me and reached for my hand. "Come on. Dinner's ready."

I took his hand and followed him into the huge dining room. We sat at a long table, like the ones you see in those old movies. I had half expected for us to sit at opposite ends of the table. But we sat directly across from each other. I enjoyed a meal of lobster with all the trimmings. Afterwards, we settled down in the living room for drinks.

I sat on the sofa and watched as Kwame flipped through a pile of CD's. "You like jazz?" he asked.

"I do," I replied.

He smiled. "Good, I don't have much gospel."

I shook my head. "I listen to more than just gospel, Kwame."

He shrugged. "I wasn't sure. I didn't want to offend you or anything."

"I'm not that easily offended. There's more to me than you think."

He put a CD in the stereo, and Kenny G began to play his saxophone. "Tell me about you," he said. He took a seat next to me and looked me straight in the eye. His nearness was unnerving. He made me feel things I didn't want to feel. He made me feel like I could fall in love with him. Apollo had hurt me, and I was scared.

"Um...well...I...uh...like all kinds of music, except for gangster rap or anything obscene," I finally managed to stammer.

"Ok, so that means you like about five percent of my stuff," he said with a smile.

"Really?" I asked.

"No, I'm kidding. I've worked on some raunchy stuff, but not that much."

"Kwame, I don't want to seem slow...but I didn't realize a person could make this kind of money being a producer."

He cocked his head to the side and grinned. "What kind of money?"

"*Your* kind of money. You've got your own studio, homes in two countries and a jet. You've done really well."

He shrugged. "I guess I have. I've produced some pretty big hits. Now, I can name my price, and people are willing to pay it."

"I can't believe that the record company was willing to pay you to produce my entire album. That had to cost a lot. They don't usually spend that kind of money on a gospel artist unless you're Kirk Franklin or somebody."

He smiled at me sweetly. "I did it for free."

I frowned. "You did what for free?"

"I produced your album free of charge."

I was genuinely shock. With wide eyes I said, "What?! Why?"

"It's my way of giving back. I owe God so much. My Mama always said that you have to give back. She said that God blesses you so that you can bless someone else."

"Wow, I...I don't know what to say. Thank you."

"You're most welcome."

We sat there and listened to the music for a while. I tried to let what he'd told me sink in. Maybe Kwame was too good to be true. Maybe he was just too good for me. Maybe I was too messed up for him. From time to time, I still thought about Apollo. I could still smell his scent and feel his touch. Part of me missed what we had, even though it was one-sided. I closed my eyes and tried to wipe Apollo out of my mind.

Kwame stood from the sofa and reached for my hand. "Tony, dance with me," he said softly.

I smiled at him as he led me through the living room and out onto the patio. It was nice outside. Not too warm or too cool. It was comfortable early spring weather. He took me into his arms, and we began to sway to the music. I laid my head on his shoulder and closed my eyes. The song ended, and we continued to dance as the next one began. A few seconds later, I felt a light sprinkling of rain on the side of my face.

I lifted my head and looked at Kwame. He smiled at me. "It's raining," I said.

"Yeah, I like the rain. Don't you?"

I shrugged. "I never thought about it."

He pulled me closer. "People curse the rain and run to get out of it. Rain is a blessing. Let's soak it all up," he whispered in my ear.

I nodded and rested my head on his shoulder again. The rain continued to fall, growing from a light sprinkling to a shower. It felt good—no—*liberating*. It felt like all of my anxiety and worry was being washed away.

"I like the rain, too," I said.

"I bet that there are a lot more things you'd like if you'd let yourself experience them," he said.

He leaned in and kissed me softly on the lips. When our lips parted, he smiled. We stood and looked at each other for a moment, and then he leaned in and kissed me again. This time I wrapped arms around him and kissed him back. He moved his hands from my face to my waist and gripped me tightly. We kissed for a long while. It felt good. *He* felt good.

He released me and pulled my hand to his lips and kissed it. I moved closer to him and kissed his lips. He pulled me so close to him that I could feel his heart beat. I relaxed against him. He felt almost familiar, like I'd known him for years. Maybe I *had* known him on a more spiritual level. Maybe the thought of him was always in my mind and my heart. I felt like I really could fall in love with him. Maybe I already *was* falling in love with him. He took my hand and led me up the winding staircase, past his family photos and award plaques, to his bedroom. I followed him.

20

"Livin"

I WOKE UP WITH A START. *WHERE AM I?* I PEERED AROUND the dark room. The window across the room allowed just a sliver of moonlight to creep in. Then I realized where I was. I moved to sit up and Kwame tightened his grip on my waist. I placed my hand over his. I remembered what happened. I remembered how gentle he'd been with me. How he'd made me feel. It had been wonderful, he'd been *incredible*, but I felt horrible about it.

What was wrong with me? What in the world was I doing? I eased his arm off of my body and slid out of the bed. I tip-toed around the room and gathered my clothes. I quietly dressed and with my shoes and purse in hand, slowly opened the door. I'd made it to the bottom of the stairs when I heard his voice.

"Where are you going?" I looked up to see Kwame standing at the top of the stairs in his crisp white boxers which looked even whiter against his dark skin.

Darn! "Um, I was gonna call the driver. I need to get back to the hotel."

He began to descend the stairs. "You were just gonna leave without telling me?" he asked.

I fumbled with my purse strap. "I didn't...I didn't want to wake you," I stammered.

He stood in front of me, cupped my face in his hands, and kissed me. I moved back. He frowned and said, "What's wrong, baby?"

I felt tears forming in my eyes. "I shouldn't be here. This was wrong. I don't know what I'm doing anymore."

"I'm sorry. I wanted you. I thought you wanted me, too."

The tears began to fall. "I did. It's just that I don't do stuff like this. I barely know you. The only other man I've ever been with was my husband. Lord, help me."

He wiped my cheek with his hand. "Ok, I'm really sorry. Stay and talk to me. Don't go like this."

I shook my head. "I need to go and clear my head."

"Well, at least let me drive you to the hotel."

I agreed. It was the middle of the night, and it wouldn't make sense to call the car service at that hour. We made the short trip from Newport News to Hampton in silence. I was so confused at that point. All I could do was to close my eyes and try to remember to breathe.

Kwame walked me to my room. "Can I come in for a minute? I wanna tell you something."

I let him in. I stood before him with my arms folded across my chest. "What is it?"

"Sit down with me." I followed him to the small sofa in my suite and sat down next to him.

He grasped my hand. "I didn't mean to upset you. You're not a one-night stand to me. I care very much for you. I'd like for us to keep in touch and see where this can go."

I shook my head. "See where this can go? I don't think that's a good idea. I mean, my mind is kinda scattered right now. I'm just so confused."

"You've been through a lot, with the divorce and all. I understand that, but I've gotta be truthful with you. I'm not ready or willing to let you go. I think I'm falling for you."

"Kwame, I—"

"I'm just asking for a chance, Tony. *One chance.*"

"How do we do this? I've never really dated before. I kind of just met my ex-husband and married him."

"We call each other and visit each other. We get to know each other."

"Okay, I guess...I don't know."

He smiled and kissed me softly. "We'll take it slow. I'll let you get ready for your trip home. Call me when you get there."

I nodded and watched him walk out the door.

♪♪♪

I'd been home for two weeks and no, I hadn't called Kwame. I just couldn't. I was so wracked with guilt over having had sex with him. I'd been putting in some prayer overtime. I'd fasted for three days and begged God for forgiveness. I was a gospel singer, for goodness' sake. It was bad enough that I was divorced. Now I'd added fornication to my list of issues. I liked Kwame, but if being with him meant I couldn't control myself, I couldn't be with him.

I sat in my bedroom and shook my head. My phone rang. I checked the caller ID. It was Kwame again. He'd called every day since I'd made it back home. I hadn't answered any of his calls. I couldn't. It was for the best that things just ended. There was no future for us. Things had started out on bad terms. We'd sinned, and there was no changing that.

AJ and Beka were coming home for the weekend, and I'd be glad to see them. It was lonely being in that big house. I was thinking of selling it and maybe moving to Atlanta. There was really nothing keeping me in Little Rock. Arkansas was Apollo's home. AJ and Rebekah were both attending colleges out of state. They could visit me in Atlanta just as well as Little Rock.

Beka was doing pretty well. She and Keith had decided to finish out the semester and then get married. She'd travel with him to his summer internship, and then they'd settle in Tennessee so that they could both finish school after the baby was born. She seemed pretty happy about things, and I was relieved that everything was working out for them.

AJ was still AJ. He'd call but he never had much to say. I worried about him sometimes. I prayed for him often. He was a good kid. He just needed to find his way, and he needed to forgive his father. I prayed that he would.

I'd been keeping in touch with my sisters, too. I was so glad to have them back in my life. I had Kwame to thank for that.

Kwame. I missed him. Sometimes I could still smell his cologne and if I closed my eyes, I could see his smile, braces and all. I could still feel his touch. *Maybe I should call him back.* I shook my head at the thought. I couldn't open that door again.

21

"I'll Take You There"

MY RECORD LABEL WAS THROWING ME A BIG ALBUM release party in Atlanta. The who's who of gospel music would be there as well as my family and friends. Kwame would be there, too. I hadn't seen him or spoken to him in more than a month. I knew he'd be mad at me. Maybe that was for the best. If he was mad at me, he wouldn't pursue me. That would make life easier for me.

I arrived at the hotel ballroom hand in hand with my date, AJ. I mingled with the crowd and had a pretty good time. Songs from the new CD played over the speakers in the room constantly, and I was receiving rave reviews. I gave all of the credit to Kwame, because he honestly deserved it. An hour into the party, I'd managed not to see him, and I was relieved.

As a special surprise for my guests, I was singing a couple of songs from the CD at the party, including the one I'd recorded with my sisters. It wasn't until I hit the stage to perform that I spotted Kwame. He was standing toward the back of the room, looking incredible in a black tuxedo and bow tie. His hair was pulled back into a neat pony tail. On his arm was a gorgeous, exotic-looking woman in a short red cocktail dress. I looked down at the modest cream dress I wore. It was a nice empire-waist dress that hid the pudge in my stomach that remained from having two kids within eighteen months' time. I looked nice, but that girl with Kwame looked absolutely fabulous.

Okay, so I can admit that I was more than a little jealous. My feelings were hurt. How could he bring another woman to my party? *My* party! What happened to him falling for me? I guess he got over me pretty quickly. *Whatever.* I didn't like him all that much anyway.

I'm a professional, so I sang like nothing was bothering me. I was singing to God, and I had no problem doing that, but by the time my short set was over, I was ready to pour a full bottle of champagne over Kwame the Swami's head. The whole time I was up there singing, he had his arm around that woman's waist. He stared at me the entire time. I guess he wanted me to see what he was doing. Well, I saw, and I didn't appreciate it.

After I left the stage, I worked my way through the crowd again, accepting well wishes from friends and peers. I finally made it outside the ballroom to the hotel's lobby. I just needed to get out of there for a minute. I needed some air. I sat on one of the round sofas and closed my eyes.

"Hi," a voice said. "I thought you'd dropped off the face of the earth or something." I opened my eyes to see that Kwame was standing before me.

I rolled my eyes. "Mmhmm. Well, I see you weren't *too* concerned." I said the words before I knew it. They just came out.

Kwame frowned. "What are you talking about?"

I stood up and faced him. My high-heel shoes put me an inch taller than him. "I'm talking about your little date. I can't believe you had the nerve to come up in here with another woman on your arm after what we've meant to each other." Yep, I was mad, and now he knew it.

With a shocked expression on his face, he said, "Well, damn, Tony! I called and called. You ignored me. It's been *weeks*. I thought it was over," he said, raising his voice. I think that was the first time I ever heard him raise his voice.

"It is. I'm just saying. You didn't have to come up in here with her, rubbing all up on her. It's disrespectful."

He stared at me for a second, and then he laughed.

"It's not funny," I said.

"Yeah it is. You've been ignoring me for weeks, and now you have the nerve to be jealous of Anya. You are something else, Tonya Langford."

I glared at him. "Anya, huh? That's her name?"

He moved closer to me. So close that I could feel his breath on my face. "Yeah, Anya Abbott. She's a model."

"Mmhmm. I forgot how you love those models. So she's the flavor of the month? What? You planning on having a baby with her, too?" I was acting a fool, but I was hurt. He shouldn't have brought her.

He laughed again. He threw his head back and laughed like I had told him the funniest joke he'd ever heard.

"What are you laughing at, Kwame? I don't see anything funny. You disrespected me!"

He stopped laughing, placed his hands on my arms, looked me in the eye, and started laughing again. I rolled my eyes. "Ugh!" I tried to snatch away from him. He held onto me and then pulled me into a kiss. I kept trying to pull away from him but soon gave in. I wrapped my arms around him, and he pulled me closer. I guess I forgot I was mad at him.

"I still don't see what was so funny," I said after our kiss had ended.

He smiled. "*You are.* You're jealous. Here I was thinking that maybe you didn't care about me, and you're actually jealous!" He kissed my cheek. "I missed you. Why didn't you call?"

I shrugged. "I don't know. I was upset about what we did."

"You mean the sex? Mm, I've been dreaming about it ever since—"

I shushed him. "Keep it down. I'm releasing a gospel CD, remember? I have an image to maintain," I whispered.

He backed away a little and eyed me. "So, I'm not a part of that image?"

I shook my head. "I didn't say that. It was just wrong for us to have sex. Okay?"

"Well, if you don't wanna have sex, all you had to do was tell me. I can hear and comprehend very well. I know you're a good girl. That's what I like about you."

"Well, what if it happens again?"

"If you don't want it to happen again, it won't happen again. I promise."

"What about Anya?"

He smiled widely. "Anya? What about her?"

I sighed, feeling a little frustrated and more than a little foolish. "You know what I mean, Kwame."

He pulled me closer to him. "There's nothing between us. We're friends, and she agreed to be my date tonight. Truth is, I can't get you off my mind, Tony. I was kinda hurt when you wouldn't answer my calls. I've really missed you." He rubbed his hand down my back. "I thought we were on our way to something good."

I looked him in the eye. "You mean like a relationship?"

He kissed me softly on the lips. "Mmhmm."

I glanced around the lobby. "Look, this is not the place for this. I need to get back in there."

"Okay, but you have to promise me that I can see you later."

"Alright."

22

"Look At Me"

I SAT IN A CORNER OF THE BALLROOM AND WATCHED AS the last of the party attendees left. I was to meet Kwame in his room upstairs. I was a nervous wreck when Tennille came over and stood by me.

"Well, we're all leaving. You riding with us back to Mama's?"

"Um, no. I'm meeting Kwame."

She smiled. "Oh yeah? I saw him tonight. He never took his eyes off of you. He's got it bad."

"Tennille, we had sex—together—Kwame and me," I whispered.

"You what?!"

I shook my head. "Shh! I know, I know. And it was good sex, no, it was *wonderful* sex! I've never experienced anything like it before in my life. It was the best—"

"Okay, okay, enough with the descriptions. I'm man-less, remember?"

"I'm sorry. I feel terrible about it. He wants to try at having a relationship. I don't know if I'm ready for that *or* him."

With raised eyebrows, Tennille said, "Wow, okay, so he wants a real relationship?'

"Yes, Tennille. I mean, what kind of relationship starts out like that?"

Tennille shrugged. "Honestly, probably a lot of them."

"Well, I know that, but how good can a relationship with him be if we've already started out in sin?"

"Tony, did you have sex with Apollo before you two were married?"

"No."

"And yet, it didn't last, did it? It's not necessarily how things start out that matters. I think it's more important how you two feel about each other. As long as you have mutual respect and an understanding of what's acceptable, then I think you can make it."

I smiled up at her. "How'd you get so smart?"

"Girl, I've taken so many relationship classes and done so many Bible studies preparing for my future husband, I *should* know this stuff."

"You're gonna be a great wife, Nill."

"I sure hope so."

I knocked on the door to Suite 103 and held my breath. I cared about

Kwame Kane. I could easily love him. I think that's what I was afraid of, loving him and being in love with him, or even more so, being hurt by him. If I opened my heart enough to love him, then what was to stop him from hurting me?

He opened the door and took my hand, pulling me inside. He closed the door behind me and pulled me into a kiss. I melted against him. I could never grow tired of being in his arms.

He ended the kiss and guided me to the small sofa where he sat down beside me. He held onto my hand and smiled at me. "I'm glad you came."

"Mmhmm. Where's Anya?" I was only half-joking. The image of him with her still upset me a little.

His smile widened. "Still on Anya, huh? I suppose she's in her own hotel room. I haven't talked to her since the party."

"Humph."

He placed his hand on my cheek. "Aw, now. Is my Tony still a little jealous? Hmm?" He kissed me on the cheek then burst into laughter.

I sighed. "My feelings are not funny, *Clin-ton*."

He squeezed his eyes shut. "Ouch, that hurt. You went for the jugular with my legal name. I'm sorry, Tony. Truth is, I'm flattered. I'm glad you care enough to be jealous."

"Mmhmm."

"I'm serious. But, listen, you shouldn't be jealous of her. I'm nuts about you. I'm glad to know you care about me, too."

"I do care. I care a lot. I'm just…I'm just afraid."

"Don't be. We can take this as slow as you want. Just don't shut me out like that again. I was hurt, you know."

"I'm sorry. I guess I thought I was doing the right thing."

He leaned in close to me. "The right thing is for us to be together. We make beautiful music together inside *and* outside of the studio."

I placed my hand on his chest and pushed him back a little. "Ok, but first we need some ground rules."

He nodded. "I'm listening."

"No more making music outside the studio, if you know what I mean. No matter how weak I get, you *cannot* take advantage of that weakness."

He leaned in and brushed his lips against my neck. Every nerve in my body was standing at attention. "You're weak for me? Really?" he said huskily.

"*Kwame*," I said, feeling more than a little frustrated.

He took his fingertip and brushed it against my cheek. "Well, are you?"

I cleared my throat and shifted my body a little. I craned my neck and looked him in the eye. "I'm *very* weak for you, and you're a cruel man."

He kissed me. "Okay, I'm sorry," he said. He backed away from me a little. I took a deep breath and released it.

"Anything else?" He asked.

"Actually, there *is* something else. I don't ever want to see you with that Anya woman again or any other woman for that matter. What kind of name is that for a black woman anyway? *Anya.*"

He stifled a laugh and nodded again. "Okay. No more Anya. Anything else? "

"Well, I guess that's it."

"Since we're talking about dates, what about your date? That was a big, tall dude I saw you with. What's up with him?"

"That was my son, AJ. I should've introduced y'all, but I was a little upset about you and *Anya.*"

Kwame smirked. He was loving this whole jealousy thing. "Mmhmm. So, he must look like his father, huh?" he asked.

"Yeah, he's just like him."

"So, your ex is a big, tall dude, too? That's what I'm competing with?"

"Believe me, there's no competition. You win—hands down."

"I don't know with the way you been iggin' me and all…"

I kissed his cheek. "I'm sorry. Really I am."

He smiled. "Okay. Well, since we're laying down rules, I have some of my own, Ms. Tony."

"Alright."

"First, never shut me out again. I'm not gonna hurt you, alright?"

I nodded. "Alright."

"Second, you can't wear heels when we're out together. It makes me look short. I mean, I know you're used to big, tall dudes and all…"

I moved closer to him and laid my head on his shoulder. "Aw, I like your height, Mr. Kane."

He raised his eyebrows and looked at me.

"Okay," I said. "Anything else?"

"Don't ever call me Clinton again."

"I let you call me Tony."

"Okay, you can call me Clinton—in private—*only*."

"I guess. Anything else, sir?"

"Nope, I think that's it."

"Good, that's enough."

He kissed me again, and I kissed him back.

23

"Desperate"

I WAS SITTING AT MY DINING ROOM TABLE BROWSING THE internet with three different browser tabs open on my laptop. One listed real estate agents in Little Rock. The second listed available condos in Atlanta. On the third, was Kwame's Wikipedia page. It'd been a couple of weeks since the album release party. In that time, I'd done a couple of telephone interviews with radio stations and performed at a women's conference in St. Louis. Next on my schedule was an appearance on the Bobby Jones Gospel show. Kwame and I had stayed in touch through phone calls and text messages. I was feeling pretty happy, I must say.

I had just about decided to move to Atlanta, hence the research, and well, I just liked learning about Kwame, hence *that* research. I clicked the mouse and continued to read up on my guy.

Forty-two years old…only son of Jamaican immigrants…

valedictorian of graduating high school class in New York...attended Hampton University on a full scholarship...dropped out of college to pursue career in music...self-taught to play several instruments... produced first hit record in the mid-nineties...has worked with stars in several genres of music...one of the most successful music producers of the new millennium...twice listed as one of Essence Magazine's most eligible bachelors.

I smiled. Yep, my Kwame was impressive, alright. But then again, I already knew that. I already knew all of the things I'd read on that page, too. But I still liked seeing it. I closed my eyes and smiled as I thought about his kisses and the wide grin that always spread across his face when he saw me. Kwame Kane was definitely inching his way deeper and deeper into my heart.

I heard a knock at the door. I sighed and left my research and my thoughts for the moment. I looked through the peep hole in the front door and saw a young lady with her back turned. I opened it.

"Yes?" I asked.

Lisa Donley or, I guess I should call her Lisa Hill, turned around with a distraught look on his face. On her hip was a chubby little baby boy. He looked just like AJ did as a baby. I raised my eyebrows. *What in the world is she doing here?*

"Is my husband here?" she asked, sounding as if she'd burst into tears at any second.

She'd caught me off guard. With a little bit more time to prepare,

I might have come up with a witty comeback like, "Oh, so now he's out cheating on you, huh? What did you expect, dear?" Or, "You're looking for that two-timing Apollo? You better check with the entire female population of y'all's church." But all I could come up with was, "What? No, of course not."

Before I could realize what was happening, she'd pushed past me, baby and all. I stood there shocked for a moment as she stalked through my house yelling, "Apollo! Apollo, are you in here?! I know you're in here!"

My anger began to build as I followed her into the kitchen. There were a whole lot of names I wanted to call her, but I kept my cool for the most part. "Look, Lisa. He's not here, and you need to leave now. You have no right to barge into my home like this!"

She stopped dead in her tracks and burst into tears. I took the little guy from her and held him because I was afraid she'd drop him, and he didn't deserve that.

I sighed. "You wanna sit down?"

She looked up at me and nodded. I led her to the kitchen table and fixed us both some iced tea. She sipped hers and sniffled.

"I'm sorry for coming in here like this. I just didn't know where else to look. We had a fight a couple of nights ago, and I haven't seen Apollo since."

"And you thought he'd be here? I don't understand why you'd think that."

She shook her head. "I don't know. I guess I was just desperate."

"I see." I looked at the baby, and he smiled up at me. I couldn't help but to smile back. "What's the baby's name?" I asked.

"Apollo, Jr."

"Um, what?" *My* son's name is Apollo, Jr.

"Apollo David Hill, Jr., the second. That makes your son Apollo David Hill, Jr., the first."

Ok, that was it. "Um, I think you should probably get back home. For all you know, Apollo might be there waiting for you."

Her eyes lit up. "You're right." She reached for her baby. "Thanks for the tea."

I nodded and walked her to the door. "Oh, and Lisa, don't come looking for Apollo over here again, okay? It's just not a good idea."

She dropped her eyes and nodded. "Okay."

I closed and locked the door behind her. Yep, I was definitely moving to Atlanta.

♪♪♪

I was awakened in the middle of the night by the ringing of my cell phone. I rolled over and checked the screen through squinted eyes. It was Kwame.

"Hello?" I said, groggily.

"Hey, Tony. Did I wake you?"

I scooted up in the bed until my back rested against the headboard. "Yeah, but it's okay. What's on your mind?"

"I miss you."

I smiled. "I miss you, too."

"Sorry to be calling so late. I had a long day in the studio."

"Really? You tired?"

"Yeah, but I got a lot of work done. How was your day?"

"Interesting. Guess who visited me today?"

"Who?"

"Apollo's new wife came barging in here looking for him."

"What? Why?"

"Evidently, they had a fight, and he left. For some reason, she thought he'd be here, I guess."

"Why would she think that?" His voice sounded more serious.

"I dunno. Because he's a cheater, I guess. Maybe she thought because he cheated on me with her, that he'd cheat on her with me. Who knows?"

"Oh."

There was silence.

"Kwame, you don't think I'd do that, do you?"

"Huh? Um, no."

"You do, don't you? Look, you can rest assured that that would never happen. I wouldn't mess with Apollo again if he was the last man on earth."

"Yeah, I know you wouldn't. The whole thing is just weird, though."

"I know. That's why I finally decided to put my house on the market. I'm moving to Atlanta as soon as I can."

"Good." He paused and then said, "I was thinking. Aren't you getting ready to shoot the video for 'To You' with your sisters?"

"Yeah, next week. We're shooting in New York. The director wants to shoot the whole thing in Times Square."

"Great. Um, I thought up this little rap intro I could do for the song, and I was thinking that maybe I could add it to the single and appear in the video with you guys since I'm free next week."

I smiled as I thought about my vow to never let him "jump around" in one of my videos. I held back my laughter as I said, "Really?"

"Really. And I know what you're thinking, but I promise not to act a fool like in my other videos. I'll be civilized and gospel-like."

"Gospel-like huh? Well, Mr. Swami, I'd be absolutely delighted for you to appear in my video with me. *And* I'll be so glad to see you, too."

I could hear his smile as he said, "Yeah, me too. Well, I better let you get some rest."

"Okay, good night, Kwame."

"Good night, sweet Tony."

I woke up the next morning and called a realtor. By that afternoon, my house was on the market. A little later, I was on the phone with a realtor in Atlanta when my doorbell rang. I answered it this time without checking the peep hole. It was Apollo.

24

"Just Wanna Say"

I LOOKED BEHIND HIM, HALF-EXPECTING TO SEE LISA
standing there. But he was alone. I stood there for a minute and
looked at him. I hadn't seen Apollo in months. He looked good.
There's no sense in denying that. My stomach began to churn with
anxiety. I finally managed to speak. But, "Apollo?" was all I was
able to say. I almost sounded like I didn't recognize him.

"Hey. How you been?" he asked.

I frowned. Had he seriously showed up at my front door to make
small talk? "I'm good. What is it?"

He smiled that lopsided grin that used to make my heart flutter.
"Aw now. Why're you being mean to me? I just wanted to check on
you and see how you're doing."

"Ok, you did. So, bye." I tried to close the door, but he blocked it
with his hand.

"Look," I said. "This is not your house anymore. I *will* call the police if you do not leave."

He waved his hands in front of him. "Okay, okay. I just want to talk to you for a minute."

I eyed him suspiciously. "*Talk.*"

"Well, can I come in and sit down?"

"No. If you wanna talk, you can talk right here."

He glanced around. "What about these nosy neighbors? You don't mind them hearing our conversation?"

I sighed. "Whatever you have to say shouldn't require any privacy. You're a married man, remember? And *I'm* not your wife."

"You got a man now or something? Is someone in there?" he asked, trying to peek inside the house.

"That would be exactly *none* of your business."

He gave me a look of frustration. "Sorry."

I raised my eyebrows. "What is it, Apollo?"

"Tonya, I want to come home. "

I stared at him for a moment and then, borrowing a page from Kwame's book, I burst into laughter.

"Tonya, I'm serious. I miss what we had. I made a big mistake."

I folded my arms across my chest. "Okay. Well, you live and learn. Now you can do better with Lisa."

"It ain't gonna be no me and Lisa for much longer at the rate we're going," he muttered.

"Oh, yeah? Trouble in paradise, huh?"

"The girl's just young and silly. I can't stay there anymore. Can I just come home?"

"You can *go* home. *This* is not your home anymore."

"Come on, Tonya. Give us one more chance."

"My Lord, Apollo. You have the audacity to come over here and ask to come home and you haven't even had the decency to apologize for the things you've done. You are something else."

"Oh, yeah. I'm sorry, Tonya," he said matter-of-factly.

I released an exasperated sigh. "Just leave, Apollo, before that wife of yours comes back over here looking for you, and I have both of you arrested."

His eyes widened. "Lisa's been here? Really?"

"Yeah, she was here yesterday, acting like a crazy woman. She thought you were here."

"Is she okay? You didn't hurt her, did you?"

I cannot believe this man! Was he serious? "Oh my G—really, Apollo? Is your ego really that big? You think I would fight her over you? Seriously? Leave, Apollo, just *leave*." This time I pushed the door with enough force that I was able to shut it. I leaned against it, closed my eyes, and took a deep breath. *Lord, help me. Lord, help us all.*

25

"Love"

I SMILED AS I WATCHED KWAME WALK ONTO THE VIDEO set. I was more than glad to see him, and he looked nice in his black leather pants, white t-shirt, and black leather jacket. He gave me a wide metallic smile as he walked over to me and hugged me.

"Darlin', you're wearing heels," he said into my ear.

"Yes, dear, and I'm also wearing some jewelry, jeans, a sweater, and underwear," I whispered into his ear.

"Underwear, too?" he said and then stepped back and looked at me with a surprised expression on his face.

I laughed and swatted his arm. "I sure missed you."

He kissed my cheek. "I was just thinking the same thing."

"Come on, let's get to work."

He kissed me softly on the lips. "Yes, ma'am."

We had a ball shooting the video, and it was really good just being with him. I think my sisters enjoyed working with him, too.

By the time the work day had ended, they'd all figured out that we had more than a working relationship since Kwame took every break as an opportunity to hug and kiss me or hold my hand. He showed me repeatedly that he really had missed me. And I have to say that I was enjoying his attention. Once the video shoot was complete, we parted ways with a promise to meet again later that night.

♫♫♫

I rushed out of the bedroom of my suite, still barefoot, but dressed for my date with Kwame. I smiled as I opened the door. He looked nice in a dark pair of fitted jeans and a red t-shirt. But then again, he always looked nice in whatever he wore.

He kissed me in the cheek, making my skin tingle. "You smell nice."

I blushed. "Thanks. Give me a minute to finish getting ready."

He grabbed my arm. "Um, actually, you're just fine like that."

I looked down at the black slacks and cream blouse I wore and my bare feet. "What?" I asked.

He took my hand and led me to the sofa. "Let's just stay here."

"I thought we were going to a party."

He shrugged. "I want you all to myself," he said softly.

"Okay, so what do you want to do then?"

"Talk? Look at each other? Nothing at all. I just wanna be with you, Tony. I've missed being with you, *so much*."

My heart rate began to increase. What was this man doing to me? I looked down at our joined hands and said, "Really?"

He planted a long kiss on my lips. "Tony, I don't think you realize how I feel about you."

As I caught my breath, I said, "H…How do you feel?"

"I think I love you."

I raised my eyebrows. "You think?"

"I'm pretty sure? Look, Tony. I just know that you're always on my mind. I worry about you when I can't get you on the phone. I pray for you all the time. I can't stand the thought of being without you. I dream about you, about us, together. Isn't that love?"

I nodded as I looked him in the eye. "I think it is."

He smiled at me and softly caressed my cheek. "I just wanna be here with you, in your presence. If that's okay with you."

I smiled. "It's more than okay with me."

We spent the remainder of the evening laughing and talking. And when we ran out of things to say, we just looked at one another. It was the best night I remembered having in a long time.

♫♫♫

I sat in the middle of the floor in my new Atlanta condo and stared at the boxes and crates that nearly covered every inch of the living room floor. I sighed. I was already tired from coordinating the move. Now I was faced with the task of unpacking. I really wished

I'd given away more of my things. At least then I wouldn't have so many boxes to go through.

My sisters were going to come over and help me in a few days. Beka and AJ were due to visit me in a couple of weeks. But I was just always the type who liked for things to be in order. I wasn't going to be able to wait around for someone to come and help.

I opened a box full of photo albums and smiled as I thumbed through the photos of AJ and Beka as small children. I missed those days. Back then I was certain of the things in my life. Or at least I thought I was. In my mind and even my heart, I knew Apollo and I were in love and I knew we both loved God. I knew we wanted the same things in life.

I believed that my children would grow up to be successful. I believed that we'd live happily ever after. I just *knew* it. I mean, isn't that how things go when you live the right way and live a Godly life? I shook my head. Nothing in my life was certain anymore. I'd moved back to Atlanta to be near my family, but it didn't really feel like home anymore. My kids were grown, but I still worried about them sometimes. Would things work out for Rebekah and her baby? Would AJ stay on course with his education?

I was into this new relationship with Kwame, or at least I *guess* you could call it a relationship. When I wasn't on the road working and promoting my CD, Kwame was on the road, producing, writing, or whatever.

He said that he loved me, and I believed him. The thing is, I wasn't sure how I felt about him. I cared about him. I enjoyed being with him, and I liked the way I felt when I was with him. Maybe part of me was still a little hung up on Apollo. Maybe part of me really wasn't ready to move on. Whatever it was, I hated being so unsure of things.

I flipped to one of me and Apollo's old wedding photos. I was so young, so innocent. Now, more than twenty years and forty pounds later, here I was, single and alone in this condo. Although it was much smaller than my house in Arkansas, it was still a huge space for one person. I closed my eyes and said a silent prayer: *Lord, lead me in the right direction. Show me where to go from here and please stay by my side the whole way.* As I opened my eyes, my phone began to ring. I smiled as I answered Kwame's call.

26

"Imagine Me"

I STEPPED OUT OF THE LIMO AND GRABBED KWAME'S hand. I smiled as we stepped onto the red carpet. I held my long beaded lilac gown in my hand as we inched our way through the crowd. Light bulbs flashed almost continuously, leaving spots in my vision, and the screaming and cheers of fans and onlookers was nearly deafening. Kwame smiled and waved at the fans. It wasn't my first trip to the Grammys, but it was the first time I'd stepped out on Kwame's arm. I could just imagine the field day the tabloids would have over the pairing of a hip hop producer and a gospel singer. I was nervous, but I was also elated to be with Kwame.

In the few months that we'd been together, we'd both been busy with our careers, but we'd spent as much time together as we could. I'd met his lovely daughter and had even been back to Jamaica and visited Aunt Fefe again. I adored Kwame. I'd never said the word "love," but I definitely felt it. I loved him, but was so very afraid to say it.

My nervousness that night was fueled by the fact that we were nominated for our work on my album. Although I was sure that we'd win, the thought of walking up on that stage in front of a room full of celebrities was always unnerving, no matter how many times I'd done it before. As we made our way into the theater, I took a deep breath and squeezed Kwame's hand. He kissed me, and I smiled.

We sat through the long ceremony, side by side. I applauded Kwane's win for producing an album in the R&B category, and then we accepted the Gospel Album of the Year Award together. I thought I would melt as I stood next to him on that stage and listened to his acceptance speech

"I'd first like to thank God. I need to thank this lovely lady standing next to me, the incomparable Ms. Tonya Langford, for giving me the opportunity to produce her album and for making my world so much more beautiful than I ever thought it could be. And I dedicate this award to my late mother, Marietta Francis. I love you Ma!" He then leaned over and kissed my cheek before relinquishing the microphone to me.

It was a good night, and I was glad I'd been able to share it with him

After the ceremony, we piled back into the limo. "Where are we headed?" I asked. "To one of the after-parties?"

Kwame took my hand in his. "Just one. I promise not to keep you out too late.

I shrugged. "I'm a big girl. I can stay out as late as I want to."

He leaned in close to me and smiled. "Really now? I like the sound of that."

I smiled and turned my attention to the traffic outside the window as the limo driver navigated the LA streets en-route to Ryan Cade's Grammy party—the one party that no one wanted to miss. Minutes later, the limo pulled in front of the upscale night club where the legendary producer was hosting his party. Kwame and I walked into the building, trophies in hand, and began to make our way through the thick crowd to an empty table. We made slow progress as Kwame's popularity glowed like a neon sign. We could hardly take two steps without someone stopping him to congratulate him or exchange business cards with him. I counted at least five very popular singers who asked him about working on their upcoming projects. Kwame was always polite. He always smiled, and he was always sure to introduce me.

I was more than thankful when we finally made it to our table. I was relieved to sit down and rest my aching feet. My shoes were a gorgeous, one-of-a-kind pair designed by a top designer. I'd especially chosen them because they were low enough that in them, I was even with Kwame's height. But they had long passed their expiration date, and my dogs were barking loud

"Hey, there's Lionel Grimm. I'm gonna go and holler at him. Will you be okay?" Kwame said. Lionel Grimm was the head of the top

Hip Hop labels on the east coast, Grimm Reaper, Inc.

"Sure, go ahead," I replied

Kwame leaned over and kissed my cheek. "I'll be back before you can miss me."

I smiled and watched as he disappeared into the crowd of celebrities. I sat at the table by myself and people-watched. It was interesting seeing how these people interacted with one another. A few people came over and offered their congratulations for my win. Some I knew and others didn't, but I appreciated all of their well-wishes.

Before I realized it, an hour had passed, and Kwame still had not returned to the table. I'd had four glasses of wine, and I really needed to use the ladies' room—which I *hated* to do. I just never liked using public restrooms, no matter how swanky the place was. After sitting there for ten more minutes, I grabbed my evening bag and all of our trophies, and headed to the ladies room. I was thankful that the largest stall was empty and had a small bench inside of it. I set the trophies and my purse on the bench and went about the ordeal of lining the toilet seat with tissue, then squatting over it to relieve myself. I felt ten pounds lighter when I walked from the stall to the sink. There was a tall, curvy young lady standing at the sink next to me.

"Hi," I said.

She turned to look at me with a smile on her face. "Hi—wait you're here with Kwame, aren't you? I saw you two come in."

I smiled. "Yes, I'm Tonya Langford, and you are?"

"That's right! You're the gospel singer whose album he produced."

I nodded. "Yes, I am."

"Well, congratulations on winning. It was nice of him to be your date tonight."

I frowned. "Yes, well. Kwame and I are very close. So it was natural for him to come as my date."

"Oh, so you're friends? That's nice. But as far as I'm concerned, Kwame is way too good in bed for me to settle for being his friend. I'm gonna get that man. Just you wait and see. Hey, tell him to call me. I haven't heard from him in a couple of weeks, and I miss hooking up with him. My name is Trina. He knows my number."

She flashed me another smile and flounced out of the bathroom, tossing her exaggerated weave over her shoulder. I stood there for a few minutes. *Hooking up? A couple of weeks?* He's calling and hooking up with this…this woman, and he says he *loves* me. I was mad and hurt, but honestly, what did I expect? We barely saw each other and after all, *I* wasn't having sex with him.

After several minutes, I finally unglued my feet from the spot on the restroom floor and slowly made my way back to the table—still no Kwame. *For all I know, he's somewhere planning to "hook up" with someone tonight. I sure know how to pick 'em.*

The longer I sat there, the more upset I became until finally, I grabbed my purse and my trophies fully intending to leave Kwame to find a ride back to the hotel on his own. I was sure he'd have no problem. But before I could even stand to my feet, he reappeared with an apologetic look on his face. "I'm so sorry, Tony."

"Mmhmm," was my only reply.

He pulled his chair around the table and sat right next to me. He rubbed my arm and said, "I seem to be the man everyone wants to talk to tonight. Did you miss me?"

I moved my arm and said, "I'm ready to go."

He raised his eyebrows. "Oh, okay. You tired?"

"*Very*," I said curtly.

Kwame frowned. "Well, let's go."

I stood and began to walk towards the entrance leaving him in my dust. He soon caught up with me and gently gripped my arm as he waved goodbye to what amounted to a room full of his fan club members. Yeah, I was ticked off. Once we were outside, I plastered on a fake smile as the driver opened the door for us. I wasn't about to give the tabloids something to write about. Inside the limo, I kept my eyes glued to the scenery outside the window. I could feel Kwame looking at me, but I didn't turn around.

Back at the hotel, he walked me to my suite, and when he tried to kiss me, I backed out of his reach and said, "Good night, Kwame."

I was in my room before he could answer me. I kicked my shoes off and collapsed onto the bed. I closed my eyes and tried to chase away the visions of me snatching Trina's weave out of her head. But they were soon replaced with visions of me kicking Kwame in his sensitive parts. I grabbed one of the pillows, buried my head in it and said, "Arg!"

A knock at my door startled me. I walked over to it and could see Kwame through the peep hole. "Kwame, I'm really tired," I said through the door.

"I know. I need to talk to you."

"I don't feel like talking."

"Come on, Tony. I can stand out here all night and knock and beg, or you can let me in. I'll only be a minute."

"Ugh! Fine!" I snatched the door open and let him into the room. "What is it?"

"Well. I need to know the same thing. What's with the attitude? What happened at the club? I really am sorry for leaving you alone for such a long time. I won't ever let that happen again."

I sat down on the sofa. "That ain't even the half of it, Kwame."

"Well, then what is it?"

I sighed. "Look, it's been fun. But maybe we should end this now."

"What?! Where did this come from?" He sounded shocked.

I closed my eyes and leaned against the back of the sofa. "Look, Kwame. I've been through this once before. I can't take another round of heartbreak. I just can't."

With a deep look of concern, he said, "Tony, what is going on? What happened? Have I done something to hurt you?"

"I met your friend, *Trina*."

He gave me a confused look. "Trina...Trina...Trina, *who*?"

My eyes widened. "Really? You don't even know her last name? *Wow*," I scoffed.

The furrow in his brow deepened. "Should I know her? Who is she?"

"According to her, she's someone you've been hooking up with. She told me all about how good you are in bed. So you slept with her without even knowing her last name? That is just disgusting!"

He laid his hand on my arm, and I moved it. "Don't touch me. You disgust me!"

"Tony, listen to me, she means nothing to me."

I twisted my neck and looked at him. "Oh, okay. So *now* you remember her, huh?"

He nodded slowly. "Vaguely. I met her a while back. I think she's a model."

Of course she's a model. "*Met* her. Is that what you call it?"

"I met her, and we hooked up *one time*. It wasn't very memorable, to be honest."

I rolled my eyes. "Is that supposed to make me feel better?"

"It's the truth, Tony. I told you that I used to be wild. I've never lied about my past, but I'm not like that anymore. I haven't talked to that girl in months, since before I met you."

I shook my head. "She said she hadn't talked to you in a couple of weeks."

"Then she lied."

"What reason would she have to lie to me? She thought I was just your friend."

"Come on, Tony. Everyone knows we're a couple. It's not like we've kept it a secret."

I began to feel more than a little foolish. I'd let Lisa Donley fool me into believing she was an innocent victim. Had I let Trina dupe me, too? "She acted like she didn't know," I said as I dropped my eyes.

Kwame sighed. "The operative word is *acted*. She knows, Tony. Look, I know your husband mistreated you, and I'm sorry about that, but I'm not him. I'm not playing games with you. I care deeply for you."

I was quiet because I didn't know what to say. I really wanted to believe him, but how could I?

"Trina's probably just jealous because me and her never amounted to anything, and we never will."

I remained quiet.

"Are you gonna stay mad at me?"

I shrugged.

"Fine." He pulled his cell phone from his pocket. "I'ma call her, and she's gonna tell you the truth herself."

I looked at him as he scrolled though his contacts. "Wait, you still have her number?"

His hand froze in mid air. He nodded. "I have a lot of numbers. I never delete them."

"Well, if she was so forgettable, I would think you would've deleted her number by now."

He nodded. "W…well, that's the thing. I forgot I even had the number until just now."

I turned my body and looked him in the eye. "Exactly how many numbers do you have in there, Kwame? I bet you've got hundreds of 'hook-up' buddies right at your fingertips."

He looked startled. "I…I don't know. It doesn't matter. I only care about you."

I folded my arms across my chest. "Yeah, well, I'm not surprised. I mean, since I won't sleep with you, I guess you had to get it somewhere."

His eyes widened. He looked like I'd just slapped him in the face. "What? You're making me sound like a damn Neanderthal! You think I can't control myself any better than that?"

I shrugged. "I don't know. You must still have that number for some reason."

"Fine, I'll delete it. See."

I watched as he deleted the number and shook my head. "What about the rest of them?"

He sat there for a moment and stared at me. Then he stood and reached for my hand. "Come with me."

"Where?"

"Just come with me, Tony, *please*."

I sighed heavily and took his hand as he led me out to the

balcony. "What are we doing out here?" I asked.

He leaned in and kissed my cheek then stretched his hand back and threw his phone. I watched as it landed in the lighted swimming pool below.

I looked at him in shock. "What in the world?"

He placed his hands on my arms and said, "I just gave that number to a lot of people tonight who are willing to pay me a bunch of money to work with them, but I love you, Tony. I really do, and if that phone or those numbers were going to be a problem for us then they had to go."

"Kwame..."

"I'll get another one tomorrow."

"But, Kwame—"

He pulled me into his arms. "I don't want anyone else, Tony." He kissed me softly.

"I just thought—"

He cupped my face in his hands. "Don't think. Just feel what I'm saying. I love you."

He kissed me again. I rested my head on his shoulder and right at that moment, it became clearer than ever just how much I loved him. I should've told him so, but I didn't.

♪♪♪

I shut the water in the tub off and picked my cell phone up

from the toilet seat. "Okay, I'm back."

"Good, I missed you."

I smiled. "Missed you, too."

"Mmhmm."

"Um, Kwame, are you sure this isn't wrong?"

"What? Taking a bath together over the phone?"

"Yeah, I mean, isn't it kinda like phone sex?"

He laughed. "Um, sweetie, I've had phone sex before, and this is definitely nothing like phone sex. I mean, we haven't said or done anything sexual, have we?"

"No." I still sounded and felt a little unsure.

"Aw now, I just wanted to take a bath with you, and I figured that this was the only safe way to do it."

I kicked at the bubbles surrounding my feet. "So, you're really in the tub, too?"

"Yes, I am. I'll take a picture and send it to you. Hold on." After a few seconds he returned to the phone. "Okay, check your messages."

I clicked to the photo on my phone and smiled. I could see Kwame in his huge tub, smiling and waving at me. "Aw, aren't you cute."

"Thanks, baby. Now, that's for your eyes only. I can't tell you what it would do to my street cred if a picture of me taking a bubble bath got out. Hey, send me one of you."

I hesitated. I mean, didn't I hear about compromising photos of stars turning up on the web all the time?

As if he was reading my mind, Kwame said, "The picture is safe with me, but if you don't wanna send it, I'll just have to take your word for it."

I sighed as Apollo's words echoed in my head, *"You're boring. No life in you..."* I snapped the picture, and then sent it to Kwame's phone.

"Aw, there she is. Still just as beautiful as ever…the most beautiful girl in the world."

I smiled. "Gee, thanks, Mr. Kane. You look pretty nice yourself."

"I miss you, Tony. I hate that I've been so busy with work lately. I'm gonna try to get down there to see you in a couple of weeks." Kwame was in LA working on an album with a new R&B group.

"That sounds good, 'cause I miss you too, Kwame. I really do."

"Well, I better get off the phone and out of this tub. I've got to get up early in the morning. Goodnight, sweetheart. I love you."

I smiled. "I love you, too." I sighed with relief. I'd finally said it, and I'd meant it. I loved Kwame Kane with all my heart.

I woke up the next morning feeling good. I sat at my kitchen table and poured over the new contract my record label was proposing. They were so impressed with the sales and cross-over success of my new CD, *Radical Praise*; they were offering me a very lucrative three-album deal. Honestly, I wasn't even sure if I wanted to continue recording. Maybe I'd just lead worship at my father's old church or something. After all, I didn't need a record deal to sing for God.

I guess telling Kwame how I felt had liberated me. I felt like, no matter what decision I made, there were nothing but good days ahead of me. It was as if I could feel God's face shining on me. I finished reading over the contract, then pulled on an old pair of jeans and a t-shirt and piddled around my condo, smiling and singing praise music. I was still smiling when I answered a knock at my door.

"Who is it?"

"Kwame," answered the voice on the other side of the door.

I swung the door open and was shocked to see that it actually *was* Kwame. I nearly cried at the sight of him. I hadn't seen him in weeks, and I had really missed him. I hugged him tightly. He felt and smelled *so good*.

I held his face in my hands and looked up at him. "What in the world are you doing here? I thought you were in LA!"

He stepped into my condo and kissed my cheek. "I *was* in LA. I had to see you."

I kissed him. "What about your work?"

"It can wait. I had to see you. I had to hear you say the words in person."

"What words?"

He cupped my face in his hands and looked me in the eye. "You said that you loved me. Last night—on the phone. I need to hear it again. I need to see you when you say it."

I smiled at him. "I love you, Kwame. I love you so, so much."

His eyes searched mine. "You mean it?"

I nodded. "I do." I kissed him again. "I love you, Clinton Francis."

He breathed a sigh of relief, as if he'd half-expected me to take my words back. He pulled me into his arms, gently caressed my cheek, smiled, and kissed me. He *kissed me,* and I could feel every emotion inside of him as he transferred them to me. I felt them right down to the core of my being. I held him tight. *I loved him.* And it was more than clear that he loved me, too. I could *feel* his love for me, and it felt wonderful.

When he finally released me, he looked into my eye and said, "I want you to be mine."

I smiled. "Well, I am yours. I love you."

"No, I mean I want you to really be mine." He lowered himself onto one knee in front of me and reached into the pocket of his leather jacket.

"Oh dear Lord…"

He opened the ring box and smiled. "Let's get married, Tony."

"Kwame…uh…" I was at a loss for words. I suppose being in shock will do that to you.

"I love you, Tony. I want you to be my wife. I can't think of anything I want more."

"I'm not sure how I feel about this, Kwame. I…I don't think I can give you an answer right now."

He stood to his feet and nodded. "I understand, baby. I really do. Can I talk to you for a moment?"

I nodded and led him to the sofa. He sat down beside me and began to speak. "I wanted to share something with you. I feel like I need to tell you this. You know, my mother meant everything to me, and losing her hit me really hard. She was a true woman of God, like you, and she was a prophetess. You may not believe in that type of stuff, but I know that she could see things that other people couldn't see.

"Before she died, she'd been after me about slowing down and straightening up my life. She told me that God was sending my wife to me and that I needed to prepare for her. She said she'd be a woman of God. She told me that our love would be so strong that I wouldn't be able to deny it. Her words stayed with me. I cleaned a lot of the junk out of my life. I got rid of the people that I needed to get rid of. I started going to church again. I went to the dentist." He paused and smiled at me. "And I started listening to gospel music again. The church choir is where I actually got my start, you know? I played instruments for the choir. Anyway, I ran across some of your stuff, and I heard that voice of yours.

"I fell in love with that voice and I knew I had to work with you. Maybe I can see things too, because in an instant, I also knew that you were the one she'd told me about, *my wife*. Well, you know the rest. We made this beautiful music together, just like I knew we would. I love you, Tony. I understand that I caught you off guard with this proposal. But you see, I've known that we should be together for a long time, before we even met. I just want you to know that this is real, *I'm* real, and my love for you is very real. I want to spend the rest of my life with you, loving you. So when you make your decision, let me know. But understand this: even if the answer is no, I'm not giving up on you. I plan on loving you for the rest of my life."

He stood to leave.

I reached for his hand. "Wait...you're leaving?" I asked. I didn't want him to go. I was feeling such a mixture of emotions. I didn't know what to do with myself.

"Yeah, I told them I'd be in the studio this afternoon." He lifted my hand to his mouth and kissed it softly. "I love you. I'll call you when I get back."

I nodded and watched him walk out of my door.

♫♫♫

I sat there on the sofa for at least an hour after Kwame left, trying to process what he'd said. Marriage? I honestly had never thought I'd get married again. I mean, I loved Kwame, and I knew that he loved me. But, *marriage*? How much did I really know about Kwame? Let's see...he was kind, he was considerate, spontaneous, and ridiculously talented. I don't think I'd ever heard Kwame utter an unkind work. I also happened to know that he had other talents outside the studio as well, and that was definitely a plus. It also didn't hurt that Kwame was rich. Unlike in my first marriage, I wouldn't be the main breadwinner. Then there was the little fact that I was crazy about him. I loved him, and I *wanted* to be with him.

So what were the cons to marrying Kwame? Well, he did work a lot, and that meant that he traveled a lot. Other than that, I honestly didn't know. I picked the phone to call Tennille or my mom or Beka or someone for advice. Then as quickly as I picked it up, I laid it back down. I shook my head. *This is a decision I have to make for myself. This is between me and God.* I closed my eyes and prayed for nearly an hour. When I was finished, I knew what my answer was. I picked up my phone and called Kwame.

"Hello? Hey, baby," he answered.

"Hey, where are you?"

"On the plane, headed back to LA."

"Okay, well, I've made a decision."

"Oh, okay, and…"

"And I'd be honored to become your wife. I love you, Kwame."

"Oh, thank God! I love you *so much*. I'm coming back. I have to see you again. We have to celebrate!" he said excitedly.

I smiled. "But you have work."

"Forget work. I'm *Kwame Kane*. They'll wait."

I laughed. "Kwame, wait. Let me come to you this time. I'll come out on the next flight."

"You sure?"

"Yes."

"Okay, I can't wait! Call me as soon as you land. I love you, baby."

"I will. I love you, too."

27

"That's What I Believe"

I LEANED OVER THE BED WITH MY PHONE CRADLED IN between my ear and my shoulder. I was packing my bag for LA and filling Tennille in on my engagement. I'd already called my kids, and they both seemed pretty excited for me. I was brimming over with joy as I quickly shoved my clothes into the suitcase.

"Wow, Tony! I am so happy for you! Geez, you're already working on husband number two, and I haven't even landed number one yet."

"Well, I never intended to have more than one husband, but Kwame is such a good man, and I really love him. *Plus*, he's seen me in my 'crazy-as-hell' state, so he *must* love me. And I can say hell because it's in the Bible."

"So are all the other bad words if you rearrange the letters," Tennille said.

"Touché."

"Well, anyway, I know that Kwame's good for you. I can see his goodness in his spirit. He's nothing like Apollo. I never saw anything good in Apollo."

"Yeah, you had Apollo pegged from the beginning. I just couldn't see it. I guess love had me blinded."

"Well, you're rid of him now, and you've moved on to someone much better."

I smiled. "I sure have. Your husband is on the way, too. I just know it, Nill."

"Thanks, Tony. Hey, you know Fred, the guy that works for Kwame?"

"Yeah. He's nice."

"Well, he asked me out back when we were recording the song. He gave me his number, but I never called him. I guess I was kinda scared."

"Fred's a sweetheart. He's really a big teddy bear. You should call him."

"So, you approve?"

"Yes, definitely."

"Thanks, Tony. That means a lot to me."

I smiled. "It means a lot to me that you value my opinion. Now let me get off this phone so I can go see my man."

Tennille laughed. "You go girl!"

I finally finished packing and was on my way out the door when my cell phone rang. It was AJ.

"Hey, AJ. Let me call you back. I'm headed out the door, on my way to the airport."

"Hold up, Mama. Um, I just heard something on TV that I think you need to know."

I unlocked my door and frowned. I loved my boy, but he was about to get on my nerves. "What? You can tell me when I call you back. I really need to get to the airport, son."

"Ma, Kwame was in a wreck. He's supposed to be in pretty bad shape."

I froze. "Wreck? What are you talking about? I just talked to him a couple of hours ago. He was on the plane."

"Yeah, they said he was on his way from the airport to the studio. He's in surgery now."

I dropped my bags by the door and rushed back into my living room. I switched the TV on to the entertainment news channel and watched the footage of the twisted wreckage being towed from the scene of the accident. The reporter droned on and on about 'Super Producer Kwame Kane' having been seriously injured in the wreck. *No...no...no...*

As I let the phone slide from my ear, I could hear AJ calling my name. I felt the tears as they rolled down my face. AJ continued to call me. "Mama! Ma! Are you still there?"

I put the phone back to my ear. "I'm here," I said softly.

"Ma, you alright?"

I wiped my eyes. "No, I'm not. I...I need to go. I need to make my flight. I'll call you back."

I left my condo, and I honestly don't remember driving to the airport, but I must have, because about an hour later I had boarded the plane and was on my way to LA. I laid my head against the back of the seat and let the tears flow from my eyes which were hidden behind sunglasses. I prayed and prayed. I begged God to save Kwame. I'd lost my father and my marriage in less than a year's time. It would be too much to lose Kwame, too. Too much. *Please God, please God...*

By the time I made it to the hospital, Kwame was out of surgery and in ICU. His rented SUV had been totaled in the wreck. There had been a head-on collision. The other driver was drunk, and he hadn't survived the crash. Kwame had suffered several injuries, mostly internal. He was in critical condition. I sat next to his bed and prayed and cried some more. I loved him *so much*. The depth of that love wasn't clear to me until I saw him lying in that hospital bed, hooked up to machines, with tubes running from his body. I loved him, and it hurt. It hurt so bad that I felt like *I'd* been in a wreck.

The doctor came in. With concern in his clear green eyes, he told me that Kwame's chances of making it weren't good. They'd done all they could but his injuries were just too great. I listened as he listed Kwame's extensive injuries. One by one and for each injury, I told myself to remember what the Bible said about healing.

"He has several fractured ribs," he said.

Isaiah 53: 5—By His stripes, we are healed, I thought.

The doctor continued with, "His lungs collapsed and he's unable to breathe on his own."

Isaiah 58:8—Then Your light shall break forth like morning, Your healing shall spring forth speedily...

"His spleen was punctured."

Psalm 107:20—He sent His word and healed them...

"His skull is fractured."

Jeremiah 30:17—For I will restore health to you, and heal you of your wounds...

He said he had a twenty percent chance of surviving. *Twenty percent.* I nodded and told him that twenty percent was like a hundred percent with God in the equation. He gave me a skeptical look and left the room. Good riddance! I didn't need to hear that mess. Kwame was going to survive. He *had* to. We were in love. We were going to get married. He was going to make it.

I sat with him for as long as they'd let me and when I was asked to leave, I only went as far as the waiting area. When I wasn't in the waiting area, I was in the chapel. I wasn't leaving that hospital until Kwame could leave with me. And I meant that.

28

"Faith"

LORD, I TRUST YOU. YOU'VE BEEN WITH ME EVERY DAY OF this journey we call life. I know you are with me now, and I know you are with Kwame. Thank you, God, in advance, for his total recovery and for our future together. In Jesus' name, amen.

I lifted my head, opened my eyes, and glanced around the small hospital chapel. I was alone. I sat back on the pew and thought about what had occurred over the past week. Kwame was still in critical condition. Throughout my daily vigil at his bedside, he hadn't opened his eyes even once. He hadn't moved a muscle or responded in any way.

Things looked grim—I had to admit that. But I had to hold onto what I believed. I had to hold onto my faith. It was all I had left. In the past, when trouble arose, I'd crumbled and given up. I knew better than that, and this time I was determined to *do* better. I was stronger than I even realized. I was stronger because God was my strength. Kwame would be okay. I had to keep repeating that in my mind. Kwame would be okay, no matter how it looked.

A scripture came to mind. "With man this is impossible, but with God all things are possible," I said aloud.

"Matthew 19:26," a voice said. It came from behind me.

Recognizing the voice, I turned around with a smile. "AJ! What are you doing here? How'd you get here?"

"With a credit card."

"Smarty." I stood and hugged him.

"I wanted to be here. I *needed* to be here for you. Ma, you alright?"

"I'm hanging in there. He's not doing well, but I've got to trust God. He's gonna bring him back. I *know* He is."

AJ sat down on a pew. I sat down beside him. "You really love him, huh?" he asked.

I nodded. "I really do."

"I've been praying for him. He's gonna make it."

I kissed his cheek. "Thank you for the confirmation. I receive it."

"Ma, can I tell you something?"

"Anything."

"I'm gonna transfer after this semester."

I smiled weakly. "Um, sweetie, can we discuss this later? Right now my mind's muddled."

AJ nodded and with a sense of urgency said, "I know, but I need to tell you this."

I sighed. "Okay. Where are you gonna transfer to?"

"Bible College. I've been called to be a preacher. I got the calling my junior year of high school, but it really scared me. I fought it, but I can't fight it anymore. I wanted you to be the first to know."

I squeezed his hand. This was the best news I'd heard in a long time. "Oh, AJ! Is that what you've been trying to tell me all this time?"

He nodded. "Yeah, but it all really scares me. I mean, what if I mess up?"

"Baby, whatever assignment God gives you, he'll equip you for. I am so proud. I always knew you'd be something great."

AJ hugged me tightly. "Thank you, Mama. You always believed in me."

"And I always will."

"Can I see Kwame? I wanna pray for him in person."

"Definitely."

I led AJ to the ICU, and he prayed for Kwame. Well, that's an understatement, really. AJ sent up a prayer so powerful that I almost thought a seasoned preacher was in the room with me instead of my young son. He reminded me so much of my father. The anointing on my son was so thick, that it totally overwhelmed me.

When he was finished, he looked at me with a peaceful expression on his face and said, "Plan your wedding. Plan your future with Kwame. He'll be healed. He'll be whole again, and it'll be just as if he was never injured. Believe."

I nodded and sat down next to Kwame's bed. "I do believe."

AJ stayed with me for a while, and it felt good to have him there. I remembered all the times I'd comforted him as a little boy when he hurt. That was a mother's job. It was nice to see him return the favor.

"Sing to him, Mama. I think he'd like that," AJ said.

I nodded and hugged my son tightly.

AJ left for his hotel, leaving me alone with Kwame. I stood by the bed and grasped Kwame's hand. "Kwame, if you can hear me, I love you. I love you, and I'm not giving up on you. God's not giving up on you." I closed my eyes and smiled as the words to the song began to roll off of my tongue. "*Jesus, Jesus, Jesus…*"

I sang on, letting the words of the song guide me. I raised my voice and continued to sing with all my heart. I probably could be heard all the way on the other side of the hospital. I didn't care. I was singing for the man I love. I was singing to God. I half-expected someone to call security to have me escorted out of the room. Tears began to pour from eyes. I sang until I was hoarse—then I whispered the words.

I ended the song and laid my head on Kwame's shoulder. He lay still. I looked up at his face. "I love you," I said. I closed my eyes and repeated the words over and over again. "I love you…I love you…"

When I finally lifted myself from his bed and turned to leave, I saw several nurses and other staff standing in his doorway. There was silence, and then Kwame's nurse began to clap her hands. Soon, others joined in. I wiped the tears from my cheeks and smiled.

"That was beautiful," Kwame's nurse said, and others nodded in agreement.

"Thank you. I'm gonna go down to the cafeteria. Take care of my guy."

Kwame's nurse nodded. "Definitely."

♩♩♩

"So, what are you up to?" Tennille asked.

I gripped the phone between my shoulder and my ear and said, "I'm in the waiting area, on my laptop. I'm trying to find a caterer in Kingston."

"A caterer?"

"Yeah, for our wedding. I figured we'd get married on the beach at Kwane's cottage. You're gonna love it there. It is the most beautiful place I've ever seen. I think that his aunt, Feona, would be willing to cook for the reception, but I hate to ask her to do that."

"Um, does his aunt know he's in the hospital?"

"Yeah, I call her every day. I offered to fly her here, but she's afraid to fly. Oh, and his daughter was here last week. She's really sweet and quiet, just like Kwame. She's really worried about her father, so I try to keep her updated, too. Anyway, I want to have traditional Jamaican food at the reception, and there's this band that

Kwame really likes. Hopefully, they can play at the reception, but I have to warn you that they're a little different. They play a cross between new-age jazz and techno. So don't be surprised when you hear them. Mama is probably gonna trip on them!" I laughed.

"Uh, Tony, Fred said that Kwame's condition is the same. It's been like two weeks and no improvement, right?"

"You've been talking to Fred? How's that going?"

"We're really getting along well. I like him."

"Good!"

"Tony, stop changing the subject."

"What subject?"

"*Kwame.* Do you think it's good to be doing all of this planning with him in that condition?"

"Look Tennille, I know what God told me. He told me to plan my wedding because He's gonna heal Kwame. I'm just being obedient."

"I know what AJ told you, but—"

"It was God speaking *through* AJ. If you don't believe it, then that's fine. Just don't come at me with that negativity. I've got to believe God. My faith is all I've got."

"Okay, okay, I'm sorry. I'm just worried about you. I wish I could be there. I wish I could help."

"You can help me by praying for Kwame and agreeing to be my maid of honor."

"I *am* praying. So are Toi and Theresa. Mama too. We're all praying for both of you. And of course I'll be your maid of honor."

"Great. Now, if only my little grandson was old enough to walk. He would make a precious ring-bearer. I'll be glad when they release Kwame so that I can spend more time with my grandbaby. He's growing up so fast."

"Yeah," she said, still sounding skeptical.

I sighed. "I'll call you back, Nill. I need to call a caterer."

"Okay."

I hung up and dialed a restaurant in Kingston. "Yes, do you all cater events?"

"Yes ma'am," he said, but it sounded more like "yes, mom."

"My wedding's the last Saturday of next month. There won't be many guests. Do you think you'll be available then?"

"Ah, a spring wedding. We specialize in those…"

29

"Healed"

A MONTH HAD PASSED, AND KWAME HAD FINALLY MADE A little progress. He was breathing on his own, and the doctor was more than a little surprised at that. But, of course, he was sure to let me know that Kwame wasn't out of the woods yet. He told me not to get my hopes up, because although he was improving, there was no way to tell what damage had really been done until Kwame fully regained consciousness. I heard him, but I didn't listen. I knew what God had told me, and I believed God. Kwame would be totally healed, and the fact that he could breathe on his own proved it.

I sat next to his bed, humming a song. I'd been singing and humming to Kwame ever since AJ told me that Kwame wanted to hear me sing. I planned to sing to him for the rest of our lives together. I looked over at him, at the rise and fall of his chest. I smiled. His breathing was just as rhythmic and even as someone whose lungs had never been injured. I thanked God.

I reached over and grasped Kwame's hand. "Kwame, I know you can hear me. I just wanted to talk to you. Remember all that stuff you told me back at my condo, when you asked me to marry you? Well, I want to tell you something."

I stood up and leaned close to him. "Kwame, before I met you, I had this idea of how my life was supposed to be. I thought that I had carved out this perfect existence for myself. Ever since I can remember, I wanted to marry a preacher. I guess it was because I was so crazy about my daddy. Anyway, I wanted to marry a preacher and be the First Lady. I wanted to have these perfect kids. I wanted success, too. For years, I left my family behind to travel and sing. Up until recently, I'd convinced myself that I wanted to sing because it was my calling, but now I've realized that I liked the attention and the prestige that went along with being *the* Tonya Langford-Hill. I've turned down my record contract. I know now that I don't have to be on a stage to serve God. I can honor Him by being a good wife and helping in my community. I don't need the fame anymore."

I closed my eyes and laid my head on his chest. "I met you, Kwame, and you were like no one I've ever known. I mean, I have to admit that I had some preconceived notions about you before I met you. I thought you were this silly Hip-Hop guy. But you proved me wrong, and I fell in love with you. With you, there's no façade, no masks. *You are real.* You're kind, considerate, and just a beautiful person, and I love you, Kwame. I love you for who you are, *not* what you represent. So, I'm ready to hang up my high heels and wear flats for the rest of my life. Wake up, baby, so we can start our lives together."

Then came a raspy whisper. It was so soft; I almost thought I'd imagined it. "You forgot, rich."

I looked up at him and searched his face. "Kwame? Kwame, are you awake?"

He opened his eyes and nodded slightly. His mouth transformed into a slight, lopsided grin. I rubbed the stubble on his cheeks and felt tears filling my eyes. "What did you say, Kwame?"

"You forgot to say that I'm rich. That's one of my better qualities, you know."

I smiled. "Oh, thank You, Lord!" I kissed his cheek. "Let me get the nurse."

"Wait," he whispered as he shook his head. "Don't go. Sing to me again. I love to hear you sing."

I wiped the tears from my cheeks. "What do you want me to sing?"

"Anything. I just want to hear your voice."

I nodded, took a deep breath, and began to sing, "I love the Lord. He heard my cry…"

I closed my eyes and sang with tears flooding my face. The only thought in my head was, *Thank You, Lord, thank You, Lord…*

When I finished the song, Kwame smiled. "Thank you. I love you, Tony."

"You're welcome. I love you, too, Kwame."

The nurse entered his room. I looked up at her and said, "He's awake."

♪♪♪

A week later, I sat next to Kwame's bed and listened as the doctor spoke with him.

"Mr. Kane, it's baffling. We've run the tests over and over again, and we can't find any evidence of your injuries. It's like you were never hurt. I've never seen anything like this before in my twenty years as a surgeon."

Kwame smiled and nodded. "Well, you never had that woman over there praying for any of your patients. God healed me, Doc. That's all there is to it."

The doctor nodded. "Well, I've never really believed in miracles, but now that I've seen one, I may have to change my view."

"I hope you do, Doc. When can I go home?"

"I honestly don't see why you can't be discharged in a couple of days. I'll be back tomorrow to check on you, and we'll begin working on releasing you."

"Good, because I have a wedding to get to."

I nodded in agreement and said, "You sure do."

30

"Complete"

I SAT ON THE BEACH CHAIR WITH A SMILE ON MY FACE AS the Jamaican sun warmed my body. I looked over at Kwame's skinny legs and frowned. "You didn't put any lotion on?" I asked.

Kwame sat the newspaper he'd been reading down and inspected first his arms, and then his legs. He shrugged. "I guess I forgot. I was so tired this morning, I think I just hopped out of the shower and got dressed."

"Tired?"

Kwame nodded. "Yeah, you're wearing me out, Mrs. Kane."

I laughed. "Um, I'm not the one who keeps initiating things, my dear. *You are.* And I'm Mrs. Francis, not Kane."

"Yeah, well, you ain't been stopping me, *Mrs. Francis.* You should be able to tell by now that I don't have any self-control when it comes to you."

"Well, if you're gonna be walking around here looking like 'Ashy Larry', then I just might start refusing your advances."

Kwame raised his eyebrows. "Oh really, Ms. Tony?"

I nodded. "*Really.*"

Kwame stood, walked over to my chair, squatted down next to me, and planted a long kiss on my lips. After that, he reached for my hand. I took it and followed him into the cottage. So much for that bluff. *Thank You, Lord.*

About the Author

Married at sixteen, a mother twice by seventeen, and thrice a mother and divorced by twenty-four, Adrienne Thompson is no stranger to adversity. Not your typical teenage mother, she went on to complete her college degree and to earn her nursing license. She attributes God's faithfulness as the catalyst for her success in life. Now, having raised two children as a divorced mother, with a third fast approaching adulthood, she is sharing a long hidden talent and passion with the world. Using the lessons that life has so expertly taught her as a guideline (betrayal, abusive relationships, self-esteem issues, witnessing the deteriorating effects of drug abuse), she has created stories that will both entertain and inspire the reader.

http://adriennethompsonwrites.webs.com

Online Bible:

http://www.biblegateway.com/

For information regarding Divorce Recovery groups and

resources, go to:

http://www.divorcecare.org/

Excerpt from *Lovely Blues*
(*Bluesday: Book Two*)
Available Spring 2012

I smiled as I pulled my car onto the gravel path that led to my mother's house. Life just always has a way of leading me back home, to my old house and the memories of my childhood. Thoughts of my father flooded my mind as the house came into view, but something wasn't right. My mother's rose bushes looked skimpy and unkempt. The yard was full of stubble, and the driveway and porch looked like they hadn't been swept in ages. It was springtime, but the gloom of winter seemed to hover over the house.

Worry washed over me as I pulled to a stop in the driveway. My mother was very proud of her home. I'd never seen the outside look like this before. *Never.* Maybe she was sicker than she'd let on. I used my key to let myself into the house and gasped. The den was cluttered and there were blankets on the sofa as if it had been serving as someone's nightly resting place. The house did not smell of the morning's breakfast as I would have expected. I made my way to the kitchen to find a sink full of dishes, and upon inspecting the refrigerator, found it to be nearly empty. *What's going on?* Did Mama need money for groceries? Why didn't she just ask me?

I continued to walk through the small house, and my alarm grew greater and greater. After seeing the unmade beds and the cluttered bathroom, I sat in the den and called Reggie. Something was going on with my mother. She'd always kept an immaculate home. Nothing was ever out of place because she always made sure of it.

Reggie answered his phone and before he could finish saying hello, I'd burst into tears.

"What's wrong, baby?" he asked, sounding almost as worried as I felt.

"Something's not right. The house is a mess, Reggie. There's no food here. Something's very wrong. *Oh Lord....*" I sobbed into the phone.

"Baby...baby, calm down. You need me to come? I'll come. I'll come right now."

I wiped my eyes and shook my head. "No, I need to talk to Mama first. Besides, she wouldn't want you to see the place like this. You know how she is."

"You sure? I'll come if you need me."

I sighed. "No, I just needed to hear your voice. I better get off. I love you."

"I love you, too. Call me as soon as you talk to Ms. Mae. Tell her I said hi."

"I will."

We hung up and I sat on the sofa and prayed for my mother. I had no doubt that Reggie was doing the same thing. After my prayer, I felt a little better and decided to tidy up while I waited for my mother to return home. I'd almost finished washing the dishes when I heard the key turn in the door.

"Bobbie Ann?!" I heard my mother call.

Special Sneak Peak of the forthcoming novel,

See Me
(coming summer 2012)

Prologue

He stood about 5'11" tall. He was thin, but fit. At first glance, I thought that maybe he was of mixed race or maybe Greek or Italian. It was hard for me to tell. But it was easy to see how handsome he was. His chocolate brown eyes were piercing. He wore his shoulder-length jet-black, silky hair loose. I remember staring at him and wondering just who this handsome man was.

In a time when guys were wearing brightly colored oversized Cross Colours and FUBU outfits, he wore tight jeans, t-shirts, and blazers. His customary footwear was high-top Converse sneakers. He was far ahead of nineties fashion.

He looked different. He was *different and that's what I liked about him. From the second I laid eyes on David Moy, I was totally and completely captivated by him. I knew he had to be mine, no matter what it took.*

One

"Going In Circles"

I sat on my front porch and closed my eyes as the warm rays of the sun bathed my face. I smiled. It was a small smile, but it was a smile nonetheless. Freedom. That's what the sun felt like. Freedom. For so many years, I'd coveted it, craved it. Now, I had it and I honestly did not know what to do with it.

I opened my eyes and surveyed the yard. The grass was in terrible need of a trim. David always took care of the yard. David always took care of everything. *David.* His name alone brought back the sound of the gun going off and the smell of gun powder.

The buzzing of my cell phone interrupted my thoughts. I checked the caller ID and smiled again. "Hello?"

"Hello, Mother?" It was my son, Jason.

"Of course. Who else would it be?"

"You didn't sound like yourself."

"Oh."

"How are you?"

I hesitated. "I'm fine." It was a lie and I was sure that he knew it.

"You don't sound fine."

"Well, I am."

He sighed. "Okay, if you say so. What have you been up to?"

"Nothing really. Reading, sorting through some things, thinking. I'm sitting on the porch right now. The grass is getting so high..."

"Mother, you should move. I told you, you shouldn't be worrying yourself with the upkeep of that house."

"It's my home, Jason. *Our* home."

"My home is in Chicago, now. I wish you'd take me up on my offer. I've plenty of room."

I smiled. That was my boy. Always worried about me. "I'm fine, Jason. Really, I am."

He sighed. I was frustrating him. "Okay, well, I've got to go. I love you, Mother."

"I love you, too. We'll talk later."

I laid my phone down and shook my head. I walked back into the house, into the living room. Reminders of David surrounded me. Pictures, awards, certificates. I sat on the sofa. Freedom—I had the freedom to cry.

So I cried.

Two

"See Me"

I walked up and down the aisles of Dickerson's Bookshop and eyed the titles. Mystery, romance, non-fiction—almost every section held titles by Dr. David Moy. I stopped and leafed through a copy of *Prose and Poise*, David's first book of poetry. A full volume of beautiful poetry dedicated to me. I held it in my hand and closed my eyes. I could see David sitting at that old desk in our tiny studio apartment, his pen moving at a feverish pace.

I quickly opened my eyes and replaced the book on the shelf. I continued browsing, finally selecting a couple of classics, *A Tale of Two Cities* and *The Count of Monte Cristo*, and headed to the counter. I smiled at Kerry, the clerk. Her parents owned the store and I'd known her since she was a pre-teen. Now, she was in college and she always worked in the store during the summertime.

She greeted me with a bright smile. "Mrs. Moy! So good to see you!"

I smiled at her newly acquired eastern accent which was undoubtedly a result of so much time spent away at college. "Good to see you, too, dear."

She took the books and looked up at me. "Classics, huh? None of Dr. Moy's books? But then again, I guess you already own them all. Probably have a library full of original first-draft copies. I'm sorry, by the way, for your loss. My parents always said he was a genius. He'll be missed..."

My mind trailed off as she continued to ramble on. I'd heard those words so many times before, "I'm sorry for your loss," or "Dr. Moy was a genius," or "The literary world will never be the same." It had been a year and the accolades and condolences continued to pour in.

"How's Jason?" she asked. I snapped out of my thoughts in time to hear my son's name.

"He's well."

"I had the biggest crush on him. He is so handsome! Is he still in school?"

"Actually, he's finished his Master's Degree and he's teaching now."

"Wow. He was always so smart. Just like Dr. Moy."

Not like David. No one is like David, I thought. I handed her the money and turned to leave.

"Goodbye, Mrs. Moy."

I smiled. "Goodbye."

***

I walked to the front door with a frown. It was ten on a Friday morning and I was still in bed when I heard the doorbell. I'd been unable to sleep the previous night. Too many thoughts were running through my mind. Thoughts of David and the day he died.

I looked through the peep hole, but I didn't recognize the dark tanned white man on the other side of the door. *Probably one of David's fans.* "Who is it?" I asked through the closed door.

"Mrs. Moy? My name is Brad Coulter. I'd like to talk to you about your late husband."

A reporter, undoubtedly. I sighed. "Who'd you say you were with?"

"I didn't, but I'm with *Literary Times* magazine. We want to do a piece on Dr. Moy's life and death."

"Well, I'm sorry. I'm not doing any interviews."

"Mrs. Moy, your husband had so many admirers of his work and his death was so tragic. They'd love to hear from you. They want to know how his suicide has affected you."

"I am not doing interviews! Please leave!" I shouted. I turned and walked away from the door as his voice became a muffled blur. "Mrs. Moy...Mrs. Moy..."

I slowly climbed the stairs to my bedroom. *I'll have to start locking the gate.* I lay down in the bed and tightly shut my eyes. I didn't want to talk about David or his life or his death. Why couldn't people understand that? Why couldn't they just leave me alone?

I listened to my cell phone as it vibrated against the nightstand. I knew it was Jason. I had no other family. No friends. Friends would've been a liability to my marriage with David. I pulled the covers over my head and finally found the sleep that had eluded me for so long. When I awakened that evening, Jason was standing over my bed with a concerned look on his face.

www.ingramcontent.com/pod-product-compliance
Lightning Source LLC
Chambersburg PA
CBHW072050170626

46813CB00004B/1295